THE WOLVER

**Center Point
Large Print**

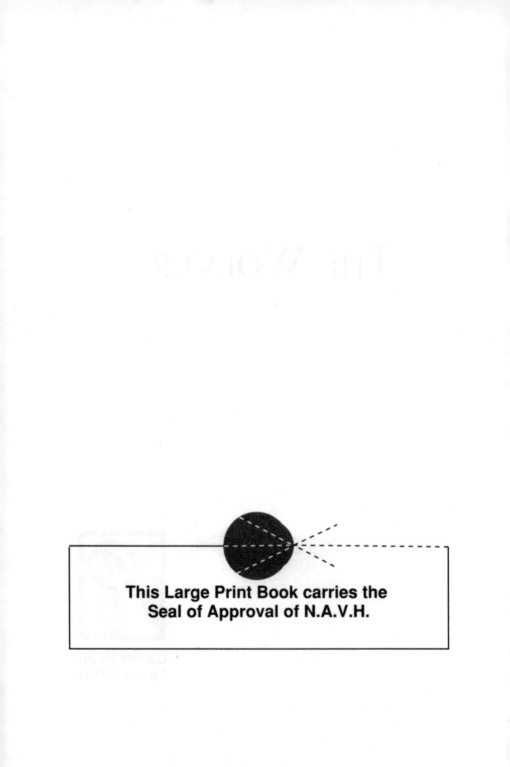

**This Large Print Book carries the
Seal of Approval of N.A.V.H.**

THE WOLVER

Ray Hogan

CENTER POINT PUBLISHING
THORNDIKE, MAINE

This Center Point Large Print edition
is published in the year 2006 by arrangement with
Golden West Literary Agency.

Copyright © 1967 by Ray Hogan.

All rights reserved.

The text of this Large Print edition is unabridged. In other
aspects, this book may vary from the original edition. Printed in
Thailand. Set in 16-point Times New Roman type.

ISBN 1-58547-830-X

Library of Congress Cataloging-in-Publication Data

Hogan, Ray, 1908-
    The wolver / Ray Hogan.--Center Point large print ed.
    p. cm.
    ISBN 1-58547-830-X (lib. bdg. : alk. paper)
    1. Large type books. I. Title.

PS3558.O3473W65 2006
813'.54--dc22

2006008750

THE WOLVER

PROLOGUE

TRAILBREAK IS DEAD.

Once it was a good town in the territory. Now only the wind drifts along the street where strong, tough men and determined women walked and dreamed and made their plans for the future.

The courthouse is only a shell, that portion allocated to law enforcement distinguishable only by the rusting, iron gratings in the windows. A charred oblong of blackened rocks is all that is left of the Valley Trust Bank. Bannerman's Saloon, a sprawling, barn-like structure where a man could drink, gamble or cavort with a sequined skirted woman remains, curiously, almost untouched by the ravages of time and the depredations of passersby.

Across the way, the sign of the Rio Grande Hotel, still faintly legible, sways gently to and fro on a single length of its dual chain, inviting those who will not pause to a hostelry that no longer exists. Nearby stands the Owl Café, its window shattered either by a pistol shot aimed in jest or an accurately tossed stone. The lower half of the bird's likeness lies in dusty splinters on the rotting floor, leaving only the over-large, staring eyes and upper part of the head to look upon the hush.

Gates Hardware . . . Selig's General Store . . . Rufe's

Livery Stable . . . The Cantina España—they and all the other once busy agencies are but fading, crumbling recollections designated by remnants of walls, sagging roofs and warping doors. Their windows, like empty eyes, stare vacantly at the world that has passed them by.

The Methodist and Roman Catholic churches yet abide, one at the north end of the settlement, the other to the south. They, too, are oddly untouched by the elements and the vandalism of man, and appear to be waiting hopefully, but in vain, for the return of their flocks.

The picnic grounds near the river had reverted to nature. Thick cottonwoods still spread their welcome shade over the dark loam as they did even before the coming of men; sealing off the sluggish stream from what had been the site of merriment. Rabbitbrush, tumbleweeds in generous profusion, dagger yucca and stiff-bladed bunch grass have reclaimed the ground once cleared for tables and benches.

Soaring oratory had been heard from the small rostrum in the center of the area: promises of statehood, talk of the coming railroad, the threat of trouble with nearby Mexico. War heroes, those dead and those alive, had been honored, eulogized, and the future had been dedicated to their memory. History was written there just as it was in distant capitals and in the other settlements that scarred the vast reaches of the frontier with their minute presence.

Yet few remember that sunlight showered cluster of

man-made structures; a bustling, new world passed it by, relegating it to the larks, the skulking coyotes and similar inhabitants of the quiet places. Utter silence reassures them and the breeze slipping down from the San Mateos tells them all is well—that the land is theirs again.

And so Trailbreak is no more—scarcely even a memory. But to his moment of judgment when all else had faded from mind, no man who was there at the time ever forgot one terrible day in a breathlessly hot August. It, too, was a day of reckoning. . . .

I

JACK SUTTON WAS UNAWARE OF THE DATE WHEN HE rode into Trailbreak. To a Deputy U.S. Marshal, forever on the move, time involved only the passing of days and nights, and little else. It was summer—of that he was certain; the month was July, he thought.

He glanced absently at two men squatting in the shade at the side of the Cantina España, a ragtag saloon at the edge of the settlement; he noted a horse and buggy waiting in the driving sunlight in front of the nearby Catholic church, commented silently to himself on the worn condition of the animal, and continued on toward the center of town.

There was an absence of horses and vehicles along the route, and drawing abreast the courthouse, he halted. Trailbreak was the county seat and the sheriff—McMasters—maintained his office and jail on the lower floor of the two storied building. Through the window of the lawman's quarters he could see a desk and an empty chair. McMasters was out.

Motion beyond the window of the Owl Café claimed his attention and he turned his head to consider it. He was a slender man, taller than average, with quiet, dark eyes and a somewhat stern mouth. The years of manhunting rode him heavily yet they did not dispel the firm set of his shoulders.

He watched the elderly woman inside the restaurant busy herself wiping dust and grime from the glass, her actions somehow giving vicarious life to the figure of the bird inscribed on the pane. Then noting two men slumped in rocking chairs on the porch of the hotel farther on, he wheeled his horse and crossed to face them.

They roused, and stared at him with an indolence born of the day's fierce heat. One was dressed in a checked suit, the coat of which had been removed and draped upon an adjacent chair. Red garters restrained the sleeves of his striped silk shirt whose stiff collar had a soiled, wilted look; an itinerant drummer, undoubtedly.

The other man wore faded Levi's, boots with recently repaired heels and a coarse linsey-woolsey shirt unbuttoned down the front. He had the browned, weathered face of a cattleman and as Sutton drew to a halt, he nodded.

"Howdy. Hot day."

Jack removed his hat, mopped at the sweat collected on his brow. "For a fact. Where is everybody?"

The drummer looked up, surprised. "Celebrating! It's the Fourth—Independence Day. Every man and his dog's down at the picnic grounds."

Independence Day . . . it had slipped up on him just as most other special dates did. About the only one he had much luck remembering was the day he had been sworn in and handed a badge: March 5, 1866.

"Sheriff down there?" he asked, looking off toward the river. He could hear the faint echo of voices now that it had been called to his attention.

"McMasters? Sure," the drummer said, leaning forward as interest brightened his small eyes. "You got business with him?"

"Nothing special," Sutton replied.

The drummer relaxed. "That's where you'll find him. Just about everybody else in town, too. Going down myself soon's it cools off a bit."

Sutton said, "Obliged," and cut back to the center of the street.

He walked the bay through the dusty canyon lying between the two rows of buildings, swung right at the Methodist church and took the road east. The sound of voices was distinct now and he could see the cluster of wagons, buggies and saddle horses pulled up at the edge of the trees along the river.

If I'm lucky, he thought, *I'll find Billy here.*

It had been three years since he had last seen his

11

younger brother. It coincided, exactly, with the time elapsed since he had been in Trailbreak and talked with Wade McMasters.

McMasters had been the deputy then, filling out the unexpired term of his predecessor who had died in a hail of smuggler's bullets. Later McMasters had been elected to a term of his own and was now in complete charge.

Sutton hadn't cared much for the man but he supposed that it was on account of Billy. His brother had been a bit on the wild side, in and out of one scrape after another, seemingly unable to settle down and pursue a normal course of living.

Jack had been in El Paso when the letter arrived advising him that Billy was in jail at Trailbreak, accused of murder. He had made a hurried trip north from the border settlement, listened carefully to his brother's version of the shooting in which a man was killed. It had not sounded like cold-blooded murder to him and so he got busy rounding up witnesses who proved that Billy used his gun in self-defense.

Billy Sutton was thus cleared of the charges and—fortunately—seemed to undergo a change of attitude. He'd convinced Jack that he was through with his wild ways, that he was ready to settle down. He had a job waiting for him on a ranch west of town, he'd said, and even before Sutton had begun the return journey to El Paso, Billy moved out to assume his duties.

The lawman was relieved, and while Wade McMasters wasn't pleased with the way things had worked out, he'd had to accept it.

"He better stay in line," the big, florid faced man had warned Jack. "He makes one wrong move—"

"He won't," Sutton had replied, equally blunt. "I know Billy. His word's good."

Apparently it had been. Jack had heard nothing from him or McMasters in the years that followed. Several times he intended to swing by the ranch where Billy worked, but somehow it never came to pass. He would manage it this trip, however; if Billy wasn't at the celebration, he'd make the ride to the ranch. But chances were good he'd be spared that chore; Billy was always a great one for fireworks.

The brief, snakeweed dotted slope leading from the edge of town to the picnic grove leveled off, and the line of vehicles and horses parked along the fringe of trees appeared before him. He roused from his thoughts, veered right to avoid the waiting equipment and gained the start of cleared ground. There he halted.

Children were playing games beneath the cottonwoods, their shrill voices lifting and falling on the hot air. Directly ahead their elders were gathered before a small, circular platform, listening attentively to a man in a cutaway coat speaking in the full, deep-throated voice of an experienced orator. Above him a flag stirred gently.

"The railroad will be the salvation of this—our—territory. It will bring opportunity—industry and

13

wealth—new faces. It will benefit us all."

It would also bring trouble, Jack thought. But he guessed that was to be expected; man had to take the bad with the good, for it was never all one way. On the whole, a railroad would help—and it was about time it got into that part of the country.

He sat for several minutes, the remainder of the orator's words going unheard as his glance probed the crowd. He located McMasters, considerably heavier than he had been three years ago—but there was no sign of Billy. He sighed, realizing he was in for an extra thirty mile, round-trip ride, and wheeling, he walked the bay to where the other horses were tethered. He'd pay his respects to McMasters, ask a couple of questions, and then head for the ranch where Billy worked.

He crossed to the left of the indefatigable speaker—now dwelling upon the probabilities of statehood in the near future—avoided the old Napoleon gun enshrined on a mound of rock and timber as a memorial to the Civil War, and moved to the side of McMasters. The lawman recognized him, smiled only with his lips and extended his hand.

"Howdy, Marshal. What brings you up here?"

"Passing through. Wanted to say hello to Billy." Again Sutton scanned the crowd. "Was hoping to find him here, save myself a ride."

"More likely be in Bannerman's," McMasters said.

Jack's eyes settled on the lawman. "Meaning what?"

McMasters shrugged his thick shoulders. "Nothing

much—except that's where he usually is when he's off the ranch."

The man's antagonism did not escape Sutton. He was accustomed to it; most local lawmen resented Federal officers and McMasters had more reason than most to dislike him. He grinned. "Good to know he's still got a job. Ever give you any trouble?"

"Nothing real serious," McMasters admitted reluctantly. "Had to lock him up a couple of times . . . fighting, breaking up saloon furniture."

"Happens every pay day—most everywhere. If it's nothing worse than that—"

"Better never be or I'll—"

Sutton's impatience rose suddenly. "Hell—it's been three years now, Sheriff. Give him his due—"

A burst of applause drowned Jack's words. The speaker had at last finished. The crowd began to drift toward the tables and the elderly orator, wiping at the sweat shining on his face, shouldered his way through to McMasters. He paused, nodded at the lawman and then to Jack.

"That's done. . . . Thankful it only happens once a year."

McMasters motioned carelessly at Jack. "Meet Deputy Marshal Sutton, Judge. This here's Judge Henry Parmalee, Sutton."

Jack shook the moist, pudgy hand of the jurist. "Was quite a speech you made."

"Make it a rule to always tell people what they want to hear," Parmalee said, mopping under his collar.

"Secret of my success," he added with a laugh.

"Railroad finally coming this way for sure?"

"No doubt now. Be a few years, however, but hope's good for a man." Parmalee stuffed the handkerchief he had been using into his pocket, and removing his long coat, hung it over one arm.

"Missing out on the vittles," he said, looking in the direction of the tables. "We better be getting at it."

Sutton and McMasters followed him deeper into the grove where tables had been set up for countless baskets of food. The women had done themselves proud with mounds of fried chicken, delicately browned biscuits, jellies, pies, preserved fruits and other savory items. A special table had been set aside for watermelons, and off in the deep shade, under a blanket of wet feed sacks, several kegs of beer awaited the thirsty.

Jack got in line between Parmalee and McMasters, began to fill his plate under the eyes of the smiling women who hovered close by, keeping the flies and other insects at a distance with wicker fans.

A well dressed man farther along paused, called to another hurriedly walking by.

"What's next, George—besides the eating, I mean?"

"Flag raising ceremony," George answered without stopping.

Sutton looked toward the platform. Two men had lowered the banner from its staff. Another was loading the cannon.

Parmalee said: "They better be careful how much powder they stuff into that old pipe—barrel's getting

16

mighty rusty. One of these days it's going to fly apart like a two-bit watch."

"Can't nobody tell George Gage anything," McMasters grumbled. "Let him find out for himself."

Plates filled, the three men found a bench in the shade and sat down to eat. Sutton skipped the beer for coffee—not that he disliked the foamy beverage, but simply because the day had been long and he felt a greater need for the biting bitterness of the black liquid.

As they ate, preparations went ahead for the ceremony. A bugler appeared, wearing ordinary civilian clothing except for a faded kepi. Two uniformed ex-soldiers emerged from the crowd, one in blue, the other in patched gray.

At that moment the children, summoned by their parents, bore down on the platform in a frantic wave, taking up positions around it. Several sprinted from the ranks, bent on closer examination of the now charged cannon. They were herded sternly back to safety.

The bugler placed his instrument to his lips and began a quavering rendition of the national anthem. The crowd hushed, rose immediately as the notes pealed out over the low hills, stirring into life a chain of echoes. The flag began to rise slowly and the two veterans came to stiff salute.

By deft maneuvering, the banner reached the top and the bugler came to the end of his selection at the identical moment. The man called George moved forward, applied a match to the cannon's fuse. There was a moment of absolute silence and then the grove rocked as the old Napoleon hurled its ten pound charge at a distant butte.

Cheers welled up. The soldiers dropped their rigid arms and stepped back, coughing a little from the bulging cloud of smoke that began to drift into the trees.

"Nicely done," Henry Parmalee commented, picking up his plate and resuming his seat. "Have to hand it to George Gage. Runs this show like an expert. You agree, Marshal?" Jack nodded.

"Can't recall seeing it done better."

Parmalee glanced up from his fried chicken. "Been around this country long?"

"Since the war."

"He's Billy Sutton's brother," McMasters explained. "You remember—"

The jurist's expression registered surprise. He stared briefly at Sutton. "Oh, yes. Wasn't in on the case but I heard about it. Seems if you hadn't stepped in, that brother of yours wouldn't be numbered among the living today."

"Just a matter of digging up witnesses," Sutton replied, a slight edge to his tone. At the time McMasters had taken for granted Billy was guilty and ready for the scaffold.

"Always good to know the law works both ways," Parmalee said hurriedly, sensing the sudden tension. "For the innocent as well as the accused—way it's supposed to be. Now, I recall a case—"

The sound of distant gunshots floated hollowly into the grove. McMasters looked up, frowned.

"Was that some shooting?" a man sitting nearby wondered.

McMasters got to his feet. "Could be some fool cowpoke celebrating on his own."

"Ben Gerlay'll take care of him," Parmalee said, continuing to eat. "Left him in charge of things, didn't you?"

Two more reports flatted through the heat. McMasters set his plate on the bench, his face still a dark study. "I did. Ed Whitson, too. But this sounds like trouble."

Motion on the road up near the church caught Jack Sutton's eye. Others noted it also. A man said, "Rider coming. Fast."

"By God," McMasters breathed in a low voice, "there is something wrong. Got to get up there."

II

WORD SPREAD LIKE A GRASS FIRE. BEFORE MCMASTERS, trailed closely by Sutton and Henry Parmalee, was halfway to the horses, the crowd had abandoned festivities and was surging after them.

Jack reached his bay and swung onto the saddle just as the rider raced in. McMasters, riding with Parmalee in the latter's buggy, paused, one foot on the step. "What's the matter, Ernie?"

"Holdup—some killings!" the boy yelled, his face flushed with excitement. "Bank was robbed. You better hurry, Sheriff!"

McMasters leaped into the buggy. Parmalee laid the whip to the startled horse and the vehicle slewed wildly about, righted itself and started up the road. Sutton spurred on ahead. Reaching the turn, he glanced back. McMasters and the jurist were fifty yards to his rear, and the crowd was strung out the length of the slope.

He turned his attention to the street. Half a dozen people were gathered on the hotel's porch. Four bodies lay on the floor. Farther along, in the shadows of the courthouse, a fifth lay sprawled in the dust.

Sutton rode to the body in the street. Behind him Parmalee wheeled in to the hitching post fronting the Rio Grande and skidded to a stop.

"What the hell happened?"

Jack heard McMasters's strident voice as he dropped from the bay. Kneeling beside the dead man, he rolled him over. A bullet had caught him in the chest, apparently killing him instantly. His face was not familiar. Rising, Sutton led his horse back to the hotel.

The crowd was now arriving and beginning to congregate around the hotel's porch. Sutton tied his mount at the side and made his way onto the gallery. McMasters was in conversation with three men just outside the door. The lawman paused abruptly as Sutton walked up.

Jack looked at the sheriff questioningly, aware of the sudden silence. McMasters said nothing and Sutton turned his attention to the bodies on the floor: An old woman—the one he saw washing the window of the café; the drummer, and a third man he did not recognize. He frowned and glanced again to the sheriff.

"Counted four—"

"Other one's inside, getting patched up," McMasters said. "Bullet in the shoulder."

"Outlaw?"

"Looks that way."

McMaster's guarded replies brought a deeper frown to Sutton's brow. He pointed to the bodies. "I remember seeing the woman—and I talked to the drummer when I rode in. The third one—he one of your people or an outlaw?"

"Name's Rinehart. Works for Selig. Only outlaws they got are the dead one in the street and the one inside."

Jack turned toward the door. McMasters dropped a hand on his shoulder. "Before you go in, Marshal, keep remembering, I'm handling things. This is my town."

Jack nodded coolly. "Sure. But outlaws are my business. Like to see if I know him."

"You'll know this one," the sheriff said drily, turning to face the crowd. "Where's Kennedy? I want him to check his place, see if they got away with any cash."

21

"He's over at the bank now, finding out," a voice in the street volunteered.

Sutton paused halfway to the door. Evidently there had been more than two in the gang—and they had succeeded in robbing the bank. He started to ask about a posse, then recalling the sheriff's remark, dismissed the idea and moved on into the lobby of the hotel.

"Ben! Ben Gerlay!" McMasters' voice, lifting above the murmuring of the crowd, followed Jack into the shadowy building.

A tall, wide shouldered man wearing a deputy's star separated himself from the knot of people in the far corner of the lobby. He brushed by Sutton, giving him a speculative look, and stepped out onto the porch.

"Here, Sheriff."

"Where the devil you been? Get a posse mounted and get after them bastards. . . . Anybody see which way they rode out?"

"South—toward the mountains," someone said.

McMasters swore. "Means Mexico, sure'n hell." He whirled to Gerlay. "Where were you when all this was going on?"

"Trouble down at the España," Gerlay replied angrily. "Was there when the shooting started. Can't expect a man to be in two places at same time."

"No matter now. Get that posse together. They make it to Mexico, we can kiss them goodbye."

Jack Sutton waited for the doctor to finish his work on the outlaw, listening idly to McMasters and his deputy making preparations for the pursuit. It would be rough going if the outlaws headed into the San Mateos: it was rugged country and there were numberless trails, all leading toward Mexico.

From across the room a voice said: "There, guess that'll take care of it."

Sutton watched the doctor step back and turn to his satchel. The man beside him, wearing a badge and holding a pistol in his hand, laughed.

"Sure, Doc . . . Got to keep him alive so's we can hang him."

The physician muttered something unintelligible as Jack moved forward. The deputy came to attention and eyed him suspiciously.

"Who're you?"

"U.S. Marshal. Like to have a look at your prisoner."

The man subsided. "Sure," he said, seizing the outlaw by the shoulder and starting to pull him around. The wounded man jerked away, turned of his own accord, and then leaped suddenly to his feet.

"Jack! I'm sure as hell glad to see you!"

Sutton stiffened with surprise. "Billy! What's going on here? You mixed up in this?"

The younger Sutton shook his head violently. "No, by God, I ain't!" he said angrily. "They think I am, but I ain't!"

"Not much," the deputy broke in sarcastically. "Caught him red-handed. . . ."

"Ed, bring that prisoner out here!" McMasters' voice shouted from the doorway.

23

The deputy pushed in ahead of Jack and stepped behind Billy. "You heard him," he said, giving the younger Sutton a shove.

Billy stumbled, caught himself, whirled. "God damn you—keep your hands off me!"

"Keep going," Ed snapped and prodded Billy hard in the back.

Jack knocked the man's arm aside. "Ease off, deputy. He's your prisoner—not your dog."

Ed stared at Sutton, his mouth suddenly hard, and then he moved on toward the doorway.

Jack followed slowly. His interest in the matter had changed quickly from one of a passing nature to one of personal concern. He realized now the meaning behind Wade McMasters' admonishing remarks; the big lawman knew it was Billy inside the hotel and he was serving notice on Jack that he would stand for no interference this time.

A burst of yells lifted from the crowd as Billy Sutton stepped into view. A man in the front row surged forward.

"String him up!"

Immediately, Henry Parmalee moved to the edge of the porch. The jurist raised his hands. "None of that!" he shouted above the tumult. "This man will stand trial—"

"What for? We know he was in on it. Old Minnie's dead. So's Rinehart and the drummer."

"Because it's the law. Now, all of you—stand back. Let the sheriff and his prisoner through. Be no lynching around here today—or any other day!"

McMasters turned his head and nodded to Jack. "Better take a hand in this, Marshal. Crowd's pretty riled."

The sheriff, taking Billy by the arm, stepped off the porch. Parmalee and the deputy, Ed, closed in behind them quickly. Sutton followed. In a tight group they escorted Billy through the vindictive gathering to the courthouse. Once inside, McMasters nodded to Jack.

"Obliged. We can handle it from here."

Sutton shook his head. "I'm staying."

McMasters' features darkened. "The hell you are! Come back for the trial."

"What's the difference?" Parmalee broke in impatiently. "Seems to me we can use him, way that bunch in the street's acting. Besides, he's the prisoner's brother."

"Just don't aim to stand for no butting in—"

"Billy says he's innocent," Jack said quietly. "I'm not leaving until I hear his side of the story."

McMasters swore. "They're always innocent, hear them tell it. All right, stay if you're of a mind—but I'm the law here. That badge you're wearing don't entitle you to go horning in."

The sheriff continued on down the hallway, then turned left into his office. He halted beside his desk and motioned brusquely for Billy to sit in the chair facing it. Jack and Parmalee settled onto a bench against the wall. McMasters glanced through the window. The crowd had trailed them from the hotel and was now gathered in front of the courthouse. The angry muttering was growing in volume. The lawman motioned to his deputy.

"Ed, you better keep standing there in the doorway . . . just in case."

Billy appeared much older, Jack noted. There were heavy lines around his mouth and gray was beginning to show at the temples. It was hard to realize that he was in his mid-twenties and not just a boy still.

At that moment Billy looked up and caught Jack's intent study. His face was angry. "Hell of a note," he said in a voice filled with disgust. "Man keeps his nose clean—and still gets blamed."

"If you weren't in on it, you'll be cleared," Jack replied.

Billy gave him a twisted smile. "Here—in this stinking town?"

"Makes no difference," Sutton replied, his words a promise.

McMasters sat down heavily, considering Billy in silence. He opened his mouth to say something, but paused as there was commotion in the hallway. Ed turned, listened briefly to someone unseen, then faced the sheriff.

"Kennedy says he checked his safe. Says the outlaws got away with about ten thousand in paper and gold coin."

McMasters nodded. Out in the street there was a quick hammer of horses pulling off fast. McMasters placed his attention on the window as Deputy Ben Gerlay and a dozen riders streamed by.

"Took him long enough," the lawman muttered, and came back again to Billy. "Well, let's hear your tale, boy. Better keep it straight—I got three witnesses who'll swear they saw you—"

"I don't give a damn what they saw!" the younger Sutton cut in hotly. "They're wrong!"

"You denying you were with that bunch when they came around the corner of the bank?"

"Sure I'm denying it. Might've looked like I was with them, but I sure as hell wasn't!"

McMasters snorted. "You was—but you wasn't. Makes a lot of sense." He leaned forward in his chair. "Don't sound like you got much of a story after all."

Jack stirred irritably. "Try giving him a chance to tell it!"

McMasters swung sharply to Sutton. "I'll handle him my own way!" he snapped. "You don't like it—get out!"

"After he's had his say," Jack replied coldly. "I aim to see he gets a fair shake."

"Meaning you think I won't give him one."

"Not thinking about it at all, Sheriff. I'm just standing by."

"What if he wasn't your brother? Would you take such a special interest then? You do this for every sonofabitching owl hoot you see jerked up for breaking the law?"

"Now, hold on just a minute," Henry Parmalee said, coming into the heated exchange. "No sense in this bickering. As I see it, Wade, the marshal's got a right

27

to be here—next of kin and all that. And he's got a point, too; let Billy tell his side of the story without badgering him."

McMasters settled back. He jerked open the top drawer of his desk and took out a slim, black cigar. Thrusting it between his teeth, he said, "Sure, go ahead. Let him tell it."

Jack nodded to his brother. "Talk."

Billy shifted, moved his wounded arm carefully, wincing a bit from the pain. "Not much to it. I was coming in from the ranch. Figured to take in the celebration—"

"A bit late, wasn't you?" McMasters observed, looking up.

Parmalee frowned at the interruption. Billy threw the sheriff an angry glance, then said, "Couldn't get away no sooner. Besides, I was figuring mostly to take in the fireworks tonight."

The jurist bobbed his head. "So you rode in. Anybody with you?"

"No. None of the other boys were interested. I came into town from the west side, same as always. Just when I got about to Main Street, three riders busted out of that alley behind the bank.

"They swung in around me. Guess that sort of spooked my horse, 'cause he jumped right in with them and started running. Next thing I knew I was in the middle of the street and guns were popping all around me.

"Man in front of me fell off his horse and then a

bullet knocked me from my saddle. The two other riders swung off and rode in between Bannerman's Saloon and the barber shop, heading for the mountains. Everybody was yelling and there was a lot of dust and smoke—couldn't see much else."

❧ Jack Sutton watched his brother closely during the recitation, paying particular attention to Billy's eyes. Experience had long since taught him that a man's eyes spoke fluently—and not always agreeing with what came from his lips. Truth or falsity—each was reflected there—and Jack Sutton was expert in determining which.

"You have your gun out?" Parmalee asked.

Billy looked surprised. "Hell, no. Why'd I be doing that?"

"They found it laying in the street beside you," the sheriff said.

"Means nothing," Jack Sutton pointed out. "It could've dropped out of the holster when he fell off his horse."

"Sure, it could. . . . And he could've had it in his hand, too. Works both ways."

"You check it to see if it had been fired?"

McMasters gave Sutton a sly smile. "Got two empty cartridges in the cylinder."

Billy nodded. "Sure it has. I used my gun a week or so ago on a coyote—never got around to reloading it."

"Yeh, sure," the lawman said.

"You smell the barrel, see if it had been fired lately?" Jack persisted.

29

McMasters waved the question aside. "Didn't figure I needed to; evidence was plain."

Henry Parmalee sat up straighter. "I want that weapon checked properly, Sheriff," he said. "See to it."

McMasters nodded. "Whatever you say, Judge. Don't know what Gerlay done with it. Soon's he's back I'll get right on it."

Parmalee turned to Billy. "You said all you're going to?"

"That's it. Ain't nothing else."

The jurist leaned back. "Boils clown to this: you just accidently got rung in on the escape as that gang was leaving the bank."

Billy Sutton shrugged.

Parmalee studied the backs of his hands. "Not much in your favor—and no proof at all. Can't expect to convince a jury you're telling the truth when there's witnesses who'll testify they saw you with the outlaws."

"I don't give a goddam what they saw!" Billy shouted, coming out of his chair. "Happened just the way I said!"

McMasters had leaned forward at Billy's abrupt move. He stared at the younger Sutton intently as though endeavoring to assess the coming moment's possibilities, and prepare. Slowly Billy resumed his seat.

The lawman relented, and shifted his cigar from one side of his mouth to the other. He jerked his thumb in the direction of the street. The crowd had not let up and was continuing to shout its demands for the prisoner.

"You think there's one single man out there who'll swallow that hogwash?"

"What they think right now's not important!" Jack Sutton snapped. "They don't have the facts yet." He faced Parmalee. "You going to hold him on that kind of evidence?"

The judge bridged his slender fingers and flexed them thoughtfully. "Like to hear from the witnesses first, then we'll see. Tell you now, though—it all looks pretty conclusive."

"Don't be making up your mind yet—"

Parmalee favored Sutton with a cool, level look. "Not in the habit of doing things half-cocked." He shifted his eyes to McMasters. "Sheriff, bring in those witnesses you've got lined up."

III

MCMASTERS WAVED AT THE DEPUTY. "ED, HOLLER OUT and tell Turley and Dave Wills, and that hostler, Sandoval, to come in here."

Moments later three men entered. Sutton recognized Wills; he was the man on the hotel porch with the drummer. Parmalee lined them up in front of Billy.

"Any of you recognize this fellow?"

31

They all nodded. Wills said, "Sure, he's one of them outlaws."

"That's a damned lie!" Billy shouted, coming erect. "Had nothing to do with them—"

Parmalee motioned the younger Sutton back into his chair, and faced the witnesses. "Claims he's not—that he just happened to be on the street."

Wills moved his shoulders indifferently. "Reckon a man looking at a hangin' rope would say most anything to save hisself."

"Suppose you tell us what you saw."

"And you"—McMasters pointed a finger at Billy—"set quiet."

Dave Wills nodded, cleared his throat. "Won't take long. Me and that drummer—Hastings his name was—was setting on the hotel porch. We heard something blow up, explode sort of. Couldn't tell exactly where it come from and finally we decided it was you folks down at the picnic grounds setting off a charge.

"Then a couple a minutes later here comes four fellers hell for leather around the side of the bank. We knew right then they'd pulled themselves a robbery and the noise we'd heard was them blowing up the safe."

"How did you know?" Parmalee pressed.

"Easy. One of them was carrying a bank sack. You know—one of them canvas bags they put silver in."

Parmalee, satisfied, said, "Go on."

"Well, the drummer jumped up when he saw them and hollered, 'They've robbed the bank!' and he run inside to get the clerk's scattergun. I pulled my own iron and started shooting at them. That sort of slowed them down and they started milling around, surprised like. Then they started shooting back.

"About that time the drummer showed up. He got off both barrels and then the next thing I knew he was laying flat on the floor. Never did see Rinehart come out—just seen him sprawled there in the street. Same goes for Minnie; reckon she stuck her head out to see what was going on and a stray bullet hit her."

Henry Parmalee was quiet for a long minute. Finally he glanced at Billy. "Sutton here admits he was with the outlaws but only because he was coming up the street at the time they left the bank. Did you see him use his gun?"

"Hell, Judge, I don't know. Couldn't tell, in fact. All that smoke and dust. I was mighty busy there for a couple of minutes. . . . I reckon he was using it."

Parmalee looked at Sandoval and Turley. "Either of you got anything to add to Dave's story?"

Both shook their heads. "That's the way it happened," Turley said.

"You see Billy use his pistol?"

"I figure they was all shooting," Turley said, "but I won't swear to it. Like Wills told you, there was a lot of smoke and dust."

"How about you, Sandoval?"

The hostler shrugged in the timeless manner of his race. "All were using guns, I think."

"He's crazy!" Billy shouted, leaping upright again.

33

"I never even had my gun out!"

Parmalee studied him patiently. When he had settled back, he said: "You've a right to ask them questions."

Billy shook his head angrily. "What the hell's the use? They got it all cut and dried in their minds. What I say don't count for nothing. . . ."

McMasters stretched and got to his feet. "Guess that about winds things up. When you want to hold the trial, Henry?"

"Ought to be soon," Parmalee replied. He turned to Billy. "You want to get yourself a lawyer, son?"

"He'll have one," Jack replied before his brother could answer. "If there's nobody around here who'll take the case, I'll get one out of El Paso."

Wade McMasters came slowly about, his jaw set. "You still think he wasn't in on it?"

Jack felt Billy's eyes upon him, bright and angry. "I figure it was just the way he claims."

"Even after what them three witnesses said?"

"All they did was put him on the street with the outlaws; nothing they said proves he was in on the robbery."

"Can't hardly be no doubt of that." Dave Wills protested.

"Be up to a jury to decide that," Parmalee broke in briskly. He leaned back, looking directly at Jack. "I'll be honest with you, however: your brother's in a bad fix. He needs proof—something to back his story. His word won't carry any weight around here."

"By God—" Billy said, with a sudden lift in his

voice, "maybe I can give them that proof, Jack!"

Sutton's hopes rose. "How?"

"The two that got away—Stinger Jones and Joe Harp. If you'd catch them, bring them back—maybe they'd clear me."

Dead silence fell over the sheriff's quarters. McMasters was the first to recover from surprise. "So you know them, eh?" he said in a triumphant tone.

Jack's spirits sagged as abruptly as his hope had risen. Unwittingly, Billy had placed a powerful weapon in the hands of Wade McMasters when he admitted he knew the outlaws. The lawman would make good use of the information—unless—

"What makes you think Jones and Harp would clear you?" he asked.

Billy stirred impatiently. "Why the hell wouldn't they? They got no reason to put a rope around my neck."

It was a possibility—actually the only one they had. And as Billy had said, the two outlaws would have no cause to pin the robbery and killings on him, once caught. Jack grinned tightly. Maybe things were going to work out all right after all. If Deputy Gerlay was successful in overtaking the two outlaws and brought them back, Billy could be freed—assuming the pair would tell the truth. Sutton's grin faded. They'd talk—he'd see to that.

"Looks like that's the answer," he said, facing Parmalee. "If the posse caught them—"

"It didn't," McMasters announced flatly, staring out

of the window. "Riding in now—alone."

Surprise flowed through Jack Sutton. He crossed to the window in quick strides. "Sure as hell didn't spend much time looking for them," he said in a hard, taut way. "Haven't been gone an hour."

"Long enough to find out hunting them in the San Mateos is a waste of time and horseflesh," McMasters shot back.

Jack watched the riders head into Bannerman's and dismount. Gerlay waved them toward the batwing doors and then turned for the courthouse. A chorus of shouted questions arose from the crowd in the street but he did not pause. He entered the sheriff's office mopping at the sweat collected on his face.

"Lost them first off," he said, halting in front of McMasters' desk. "About the only thing I'm sure of is they're headed for the border."

"They killed three people and got away with ten thousand in cash," Parmalee said in a severe tone. "Seems to me you could have kept after them—leastwise until dark."

Gerlay shrugged. "You know that country, Judge. Man could spend a week and be looking in all the wrong places. Be smarter to try and head them off at the border."

"That covers one hell of a lot of ground," McMasters observed. "All the way from El Paso to Nogales."

Gerlay grunted his agreement, again moved his shoulders. "Drawback, living close to the line. Makes it easy for these renegades to get away."

36

"Maybe," Jack Sutton said, "they'll take the shortest trail."

"That's what I figure," Billy said excitedly. "They'll cross the San Mateos and head straight south . . . end up around Carneros, on the Mex side."

Gerlay wasn't listening to Billy. His eyes were on Jack. "What's all this to you?"

"He's the prisoner's brother—and a Deputy U.S. Marshal," McMasters explained. "Billy claims he had nothing to do with the robbery. Sutton, here, believes him."

The lean deputy glanced to the sheriff, frowning. "So?"

"Reckon the marshal figures to go after them two. Just happens Billy knows them both. Thinks if they're hauled in they'll clear him."

Ben Gerlay laughed. "I can see them doing that."

"Be no reason for them not to," Henry Parmalee said sharply. "What would they gain dragging in an innocent man?"

Gerlay stared at the jurist. "You think he wasn't in on it?"

"Not thinking anything; that's what a jury's for. But I believe Sutton's got a good idea, going after this Stinger Jones and Harp. Truth is, it's about the only chance his brother's got—and you can't blame a man for doing all he can to save his kinfolk." He swung to Jack. "You know that pair when you see them?"

Sutton said, "No—but Billy can give me a description."

"I know both of them," Gerlay cut in. He cast a side-
wards look at McMasters as though seeking permission of the lawman. "If the sheriff'll let me, I'll ride
with you. Sort of feel responsible for this whole thing,
anyway—not being around when it happened."

Jack nodded. "Obliged to you, Deputy. It'll help.
How about it, Sheriff?"

McMasters pursed his lips. After a moment he
shrugged. "Sure, why not? Ought to keep after them."

Gerlay smiled again and said, "Fair enough. When
do we start, Marshal?"

"Soon as you're ready."

Ben Gerlay wheeled immediately to the door. "Give
me thirty minutes to throw some stuff in my saddlebags, and I'll be set."

Henry Parmalee gave a deep sigh. "Well, that's that.
. . . Now, I'll set the trial for two weeks from today.
Ought to give you plenty of time. Meanwhile, the
sheriff'll hold Billy here in jail."

"I understand that," Jack said. "Two weeks ought to
be enough time. If it turns out I'll need more, I'll get
word to you."

The jurist frowned. "Don't let it come down to
that—I'll have hell stalling those people out there as it
is."

"Do my best," Sutton replied and crossed to where
Billy sat. "Don't worry about this—and don't do any-
thing foolish. Just sit tight—I'll get Harp and Stinger
Jones back in time."

"If you don't," Billy said grimly, "those bastards out

38

there'll string me up for sure."

"They won't get a chance," Sutton assured him. "What do Jones and Harp look like?"

"Stinger's a short *hombre* with a big scar on the left side of his face. Joe Harp's about the same size only he's got light hair; some people call him Cotton. Thought I heard that deputy say he knew both of them."

"He did. Just like to know a little about them myself."

"You want anything else from us, Judge?" Dave Wills asked from the doorway.

Parmalee shook his head. McMasters leaned against the edge of his desk. "Reckon that's all for the time being, Dave. Be calling you in later." He glanced at Billy. "Come on, might as well start getting used to your cell."

Billy rose, extended his hand to Jack. "*Buena suerte,* brother. . . . My neck's depending on you."

"So long," Jack replied. "I'll be back."

He turned then to McMasters, his face suddenly gray and stiff. "Holding you responsible for him, Sheriff. You keep that bunch outside in hand—or you'll answer to me."

McMasters flushed. "Nobody ever took a prisoner away from me yet!"

"Then don't let this be the first time," Sutton said slowly and with emphasis on each word.

Nodding to Parmalee, he wheeled and returned to the street.

IV

THEY RODE OUT OF TRAILBREAK THREE HOURS SHORT of sunset, Sutton astride his bay and Deputy Ben Gerlay on a husky little black horse. Although his mount was far from fresh, Sutton refused the suggestion to change him for another; they were old trailmates and he preferred the big, deep chested animal, despite his condition, to a horse of unknown qualities.

"You know this country?" Gerlay asked as they pulled off the south road and cut an angle across the cactus-studded flats toward the San Mateos.

"In a general way," Jack replied.

The deputy settled back in his saddle. "Reckon the best thing we can do is head for Mescal Canyon, and cross the mountains there."

"That the shortest trail?"

"Maybe not the shortest—sure the best."

"Not interested in that," Sutton said, flatly. "I'm looking for the quickest way to the other side."

Ben Gerlay shook his head. "Means straight up and over the ridge . . . one hell of a ride."

"Take it."

The deputy hawked, spat. "What difference is it going to make? Be dark soon and we'll have to hole up, anyway. For all the good we'll be doing, we could've stayed in town and took off in the morning," he added under his breath.

Jack Sutton drew to an abrupt halt. Jaw set, he twisted about, faced Gerlay. "Let's get something straight—you volunteered for this job—I sure as hell didn't beg you to come along. If you think the going's likely to be too tough for you—head back for town now."

Ben Gerlay stiffened under the harsh words. "I was only saying—"

"I know what you said—and I'm not interested. I've got two weeks to find Jones and Harp and get them back to that judge. I figure on doing it. It means a lot of hard riding—and if you don't take to the idea, pull out now. I got no time to be bothered with you."

The deputy flushed under the lash of Jack Sutton's words. For a brief moment anger hardened his lead colored eyes, and then his expression changed. A half smile tugged at his lips.

"Simmer down, Marshal, I'm with you all the way. Anything you say's Jake with me."

"Jones and Harp don't have much of a lead—so I figure to stay in the saddle until midnight, later, if the horses can stand it."

"Hard climb—"

"Decide that later. If we have to, we'll stop at midnight, rest until morning. Got to move fast. It'd be simpler if we can nail that pair before they cross the border."

Sutton paused, studied Gerlay coldly. The deputy

remained silent, head down, hands folded upon the saddle horn.

"That's how it's to be. If it don't suit you, go on back to town."

Gerlay shifted his weight. "Like I said, I'll stick."

"No arguments?"

"You're calling the shots, Marshal."

"Then move out. Take the shortest trail to the other side."

Gerlay nodded and spurred ahead. Sutton watched him a moment and then swung in behind, having a brief wonder as to whether he had erred in accepting the deputy's offer of accompaniment; he would have no time to waste on a lazy, contentious partner.

An hour later they had reached the pine clad slopes of the San Mateos and were following a narrow path that bore due west toward a distant hogback. It was rough going, as Gerlay had promised, but the bay was taking it in stride with no apparent effort.

It was pleasant in the deep, scented shadows as they climbed steadily, and Jack Sutton could have enjoyed the passage if his mission were not so critical. The lingering touch of the day's bright heat had begun to fade and night's coolness was in the air. Splashes of red paintcups and rose colored phlox greeted them from the steep slopes, and once they disturbed a long-eared mule deer and his harem, sending them leaping away through the scrub oak and cedars for the floor of the canyon.

Around midnight, they halted on the far side of the

hogback, in a clearing where a stream cut a narrow path across one end, and made camp. There was ample grass for the horses, and after seeing to their care, the men ate the cold meat and bread they carried, washed it down with black coffee, and then rolling up in their blankets, went to sleep.

They were in the saddle well before the sun's rays brightened the canyons, and by mid-morning were pulling out of the rocky, west slope draws and turning south onto a vast snakeweed dotted flat. To the right loomed the towering Black Range and beyond it, the Mogollon country. Ahead a dozen miles, Animas Peak, a lonely sentinel in a bleak, forgotten land, thrust its ragged bulk into the sky.

"Maybe find out something when we reach that," Ben Gerlay said, pointing to the formation. "There's a store, couple houses. If Stinger and Harp come this way, they'll have been seen."

Sutton nodded, touched the bay with his spurs and put the big horse into a lope. A definite bit of information on the fleeing outlaws would be encouraging.

A short time later they pulled up before the hitchrack fronting a small adobe hut that bore the sign: BAR—GROCERIES.

"Wait here," Jack said, dismounting.

He crossed the sunbaked hardpack and entered. A man slouched in a battered rocking chair in the far corner of the room. He lifted his head lazily at Sutton's greeting.

"Looking for a couple of friends," Jack said, leaning

43

against one of the roof supports. "Figured they might have stopped by here for a drink."

"Could've," the old man said amiably.

"One has a scarred face. Other's light haired . . . call him Cotton."

"Seen 'em," the storekeeper said, rocking forward and coming to his feet. "Was along 'bout—"

The man's jaw clamped shut. His eyes narrowed and a closeness fell across his face. Jack turned, followed his gaze. Ben Gerlay, still in the saddle, was framed by the doorway. The sun glinted on the deputy star he wore.

Sutton swore silently, swung back to the storekeeper. "Keep talking."

"Reckon that's all there is to it. I seen 'em."

"You started to tell me when—"

The old man shook his head. "Was a few days ago, maybe more." He paused and stared at Jack. "You aiming to buy something?"

Sutton said, "No," and turned away. As the storekeeper settled back into his chair, he added, "Obliged to you for the information."

"I didn't tell you nothing," the man said sourly, and began to fill a blackened pipe with shreds of tobacco.

Sutton crossed to where Gerlay waited and stepped to the saddle. As they moved off the deputy leaned forward.

"They been here?"

Jack nodded.

44

"When?"

"Old man was about to tell me," Sutton replied impatiently, "when he saw that star on your vest. Get rid of it. We'll get no answers if they know we're lawmen."

Gerlay removed his nickeled badge and dropped it into a pocket. "Reckon we was right—they're ahead of us. How far you think?"

Sutton shrugged. "Half a day, maybe less. There another settlement between here and the border?"

"Couple of ranches over near Seven Brothers Mountain, about fifteen miles on. Next trading post will be the one at Cook's Peak. We ought to make it there by tomorrow afternoon."

"After that—what?"

"Nothing until we reach Pierce, a town on the border."

They encountered a lone cowpuncher searching for strays in the draws of the Seven Brothers shortly after dark. Halting, they made coffee and invited him to sit in. No, he'd seen no pilgrims, he told them, but he reckoned that was understandable; he'd been in the deep brush most of the day chousing out critters. A wagon train could've lumbered by and he wouldn't have noticed it.

They made a dry camp, picketing the horses on a sand-humped stand of mesquite and watering them a little from their canteens. Later, with a full moon silvering the world about him, Jack Sutton strolled to a knoll a short distance below where he could be alone and look upon the quiet land.

The breeze had freshened and the day's heat, stored by the soil, was slowly dissipating. White night flowers growing in scattered clusters had opened, and back up the slope of the mountain a dove cooed mournfully.

Finding a comfortable seat on a sandstone ledge, Jack removed his hat, brushed wearily at his hair and considered the future. There seemed small chance of overtaking the outlaws before they reached the border. If he then followed regulations, he would have to notify the Mexican authorities of his wish to cross the line and wait for an approval. It could involve days of delay—even weeks.

But to proceed without permission could entail even greater trouble. If the *rurales* caught up with him and Ben Gerlay—Jack sighed, considering the complications that would arise if he, a U.S. Marshal, was apprehended on Mexican soil enforcing American law.

He shook his head, drew out tobacco and papers and rolled himself a cigarette. It was a risk he must assume; Billy's life depended upon it. They would have to move carefully, of course—get rid of all identification that would connect them with law enforcement agencies; he would warn Gerlay. As plain citizens, their chances in Mexico would be much improved.

Jack sat for a full hour on the ledge, allowing the night's coolness to seep into his body, before he returned to camp. The deputy was asleep, snoring heavily.

Noon the next day found them in the wild, desolate country around Cook's Peak, crossing a long, breathlessly hot flat marked by gaunt chollas and yellow blossoming prickly pear. They saw no one, the only life visible being an occasional whip-tailed lizard scurrying among the creosote bushes and a persistent red-shouldered hawk that kept pace with them on soaring wings in the cloudless sky above.

They had ridden continually and Jack was feeling the effects of such traveling. Happily, he was meeting with only token opposition from Ben Gerlay. He thought he had the man figured out now: Ben was easy-going, inclined somewhat to laziness, and most of his protests had been pure reaction. He seemed as anxious now to overtake the outlaws as was Jack himself.

Gerlay shook his head. "It'll be mighty risky. . . . Supposing we're jumped by the *rurales* or maybe the *Federales*. Be hard to explain, us being lawmen and—"

"They won't know we're lawmen. We'll leave all our identification on this side of the line, just in case."

The deputy stirred uncomfortably. "Still taking one hell of a chance—"

Sutton considered the man thoughtfully. "Could mean trouble, all right—and I won't ask you to side me. If you feel like pulling out, go ahead. I won't hold it against you."

Ben Gerlay lay back. He was silent for a long minute. Finally: "Come this far, Marshal, reckon I might as well make the whole ride."

Jack nodded his satisfaction. "We could get lucky," he said. "Jones and Harp won't much like the idea of toting all that money across the line. Be easy to lose to *bandidos*—or to the *rurales*. They'll be taking that chance only if they're forced to."

"Meaning they'll do it if they find out we're trailing them."

Sutton nodded. "And they don't know that yet. Leastwise, I don't think so. We've never pulled up close enough for them to spot us."

"So you think maybe we'll find them in Pierce . . . ?"

"Be how I'd do it if I was calling the shots—hole up there, sit tight until I knew one way or another if there was a posse on my tail. If it turned out there was, the border would be right handy to duck across."

"Just what they'll be thinking."

Back up on the mountainside a coyote barked. Jack Sutton listened, then asked, "You known Stinger and Harp long?"

"Four, five years. Seen them in Abilene a couple of times, before I took up lawing."

Jack said no more. He was fortunate to have a man along who could recognize the outlaws at first glance; it would simplify matters when the moment came to close in. He gave thought to Billy, wondered how he fared in Wade McMasters' jail, and then did some calculating as to the number of days remaining before

48

Henry Parmalee's deadline was reached.

If his hunch was right and they could capture Jones and Harp that next day in Pierce, all would be well; they would be able to make the return to Trailbreak in ample time. But if the outlaws were not there, and had crossed into Mexico, the situation would worsen with each passing hour. The answer was to get a letter to the jurist, ask for a delay. Parmalee seemed like a fair man; he would grant such a request.

They reached the settlement during the middle of the afternoon, purposely swinging toward the mountain that stood to the east in order to approach the scatter of houses from the rear.

In effect, it was no town—just a few shacks with one larger building serving as a saloon and general store. Its existence was justified only by the fact that it was convenient for smugglers coming up from Mexico and North Americans racing south to evade the law.

Sutton, with Ben Gerlay at his side, guided his horse along a narrow passageway between two houses to a clearing that served as a street. From there they would be in a position to view the combination store and bar.

They halted at the edge of the street. Two horses were at the rack fronting the weathered structure. Gerlay leaned forward.

"They're in there, sure as hell," he said softly.

Sutton felt a stream of relief course through him. There would be no problems now; they could make it back to Trailbreak within the allotted time. He studied the building for several moments, shaping a fool-proof plan in his mind. Finally he wheeled the bay around, faced the deputy.

"Circle the place, come in from the back. They don't know me so I'll take the front."

Gerlay nodded his understanding. "Be smart to hit them at the same time—you from one side, me from the other. When I get to the door I'll give you a high-sign."

"All right—but no gunplay," Sutton cautioned quickly. "Got to avoid that unless we're pushed into it." He paused, thought for a moment. "Might be better if you wait outside—just be there. Things go wrong, then you can take a hand."

Gerlay settled back, disappointed. "Suit yourself, Marshal . . . you're running things. Best you remember, though, that Stinger ain't no greenhorn—neither's Harp."

"Odds'll be with me," Jack said. "Move out."

The deputy pulled away and disappeared behind a high wall. Sutton waited a full two minutes, then rode to the hitchrack and dismounted. Taking his time, he tied the bay alongside the outlaw's horses and crossed the porch to the dust-clogged screen door. To all appearances he was just a passing rider stopping by to fill a need.

But Jack Sutton missed nothing. The interior of the combination saloon and general store was shadowy behind its streaky glass window. He could make out two men standing at the short bar: they would be

Stinger Jones and Harp. Beyond them a few paces an aproned man leaned against a counter. No one else was visible; that was good. The fewer people he had to worry about, the better.

Sutton laid his hand on the latch, and drew back the door. Stepping inside, he halted. Stinger Jones and Harp turned lazily, stared at him, resumed their positions. The store owner watched him expectantly.

Jack nodded and moved deeper into the room, throwing his glance then to the rear entrance. Gerlay was not there.

Perhaps the deputy had not had sufficient time to get in place. Sutton considered that and shrugged off the thought. It didn't matter—and Gerlay would be there before it was over.

He turned toward the storekeeper. "Need a sack of Bull—"

The man fell back a step to reach for a paper carton on a shelf. At that moment Jack saw the woman customer. She was to his left, partially hidden by a stack of wooden tubs. He felt his nerves tighten. Her presence complicated matters; she could get hurt. It would be best to stall, to wait until she had gone.

"Your sack of Bull, mister."

At the sound of the storekeeper's voice, Jack Sutton broke from his thoughts. He reached for a coin and exchanged it for the sack of tobacco and papers which he tucked into his shirt pocket.

"Obliged," the storekeeper said. "Heading south?"

Sutton stiffened, immediately aware of renewed

interest on the part of Jones and Harp—interest and no small amount of suspicion. He swore softly. One thing he didn't need was a nosy storekeeper.

"No place special," he said, trying to make his reply seem off-hand.

"Seen you come in from the north, so just figured you was headed south. Where's your pardner?"

Jack Sutton stared at the man in furious silence.

"Fellow that rode in with you. Seen the pair of you setting out there, looking the place over. . . ."

Stinger Jones and Joe Harp eased away from the bar, took up positions in the aisle. Jack felt their hard, thrusting gaze upon him, and knew what they were thinking—that he was part of a posse, that other men had scattered themselves around the settlement. Abruptly the room was hot, stuffy, filled with tension.

He glanced to the rear of the store. Ben Gerlay was a crouched shadow outside the door. In that same instant Joe Harp also saw the indistinct shape of the deputy.

"It's a trap!" the outlaw yelled, drawing his pistol. "Let's get out of here!"

Stinger lunged to the side, seized the woman customer by the wrist and spun her about. Jack, reaching for his weapon, froze. The scar-faced outlaw jerked the woman up close. Using her as a shield for Harp and himself, he began to back toward the street exit.

"Keep standing right there," he warned Sutton. "Unless you want her dead. . . . Watch that door, Joe."

The woman, recovered from her initial shock, began

to scream and struggle to break away. Jones tightened his grip about her waist. Helpless, Jack watched them gain the door.

Suddenly, the room rocked from the blast of Ben Gerlay's revolver. Stinger's hat flew off, and rolled crazily across the floor. Joe Harp, halfway onto the porch, snapped a shot at Gerlay. As smoke boiled inward, coiling about the shoulders of Stinger Jones and the woman, Sutton rushed forward.

Jones fired hastily. The bullet missed Sutton, and thudded into the stack of tubs beyond him, sending them crashing into the counter. The outlaw yelled a curse, stepped back, and shoving the hysterical woman hard, sent her stumbling into Sutton. Jack, off balance, went down in a tangle of arms, legs and smothering skirts.

V

SUTTON THRUST THE WOMAN ASIDE. OBLIVIOUS TO HER continuing cries and the shouting of the storekeeper, he leaped to his feet. Ben Gerlay was rushing toward the door, pistol raised.

"Watch yourself!" Jack shouted. "They're no good to me dead!"

The quick, hard drum of running horses in the street reached him. He swore in a harsh, raging way, and started for the door. He reached it a step or two behind the deputy. Stinger Jones and Joe Harp were gone, heading for the safety that lay beyond the border.

"Get your horse!" Sutton yelled to Gerlay and plunged by him into the open.

He stopped at the rack, jerked the bay's reins free, and vaulted onto the saddle. Cutting sharply around, he drove his spurs into the horse and raced down the street. Jones and Harp were small blurs in the shimmering distance. Again he swore. The outlaws had been in his hands—and had slipped through. Worse yet—now they were aware of pursuit.

He heard the quick pound of hoofs behind him, glanced back and saw Ben Gerlay coming up. He slowed, allowing the deputy to draw alongside.

"High-tailing it for the line, sure'n hell," Gerlay said, squinting into the glare. "Tough break."

Sutton nodded. "Should've had them. That woman—" He paused and added, "That shot you took at Stinger was a bit close. Next time—"

"Knew what I was doing," the deputy replied stiffly. "Only aimed to wing him."

"In the head?"

The deputy shrugged. "I was shooting at his shoulder."

An hour later when they approached the border, marked only by pyramidic mounds of stones placed at quarter mile intervals, Jack slowed the pace once more. There was no point now in continuing the hard, steady run. Halting, he studied the dust cloud moving on south.

"There a town down that way?" he asked.

"Carneros," Gerlay said. "Little place. Looks like that's where they're headed."

Jack swung off the bay. Taking his handkerchief out, he spread it on the hot sand, and then, piece by piece, laid upon it his badge, identification papers, and all other items he felt might betray his profession. Finished, he looked up at Gerlay.

"You still figure to cross over?"

The deputy nodded. "Sure."

"Then pitch me that star you've got in your pocket, and everything else that says you're a lawman."

Gerlay complied without question. Folding the cloth into a packet, Sutton fixed several landmarks in his mind, and then cached the parcel in the nearest marker. That done, he squatted in the shade afforded by the bay, and began to roll himself a cigarette.

"Thought you was in a big hurry to catch up."

Jack stirred. "Too late for that now. Only thing we can do is wait—make them think we didn't trail them across the border."

Gerlay came off his black. "You figure they'll hole up in Carneros?"

"Be my guess, if they're convinced we're not following them."

They stalled out a full hour, sitting in the blazing sunlight until the dust to the south had completely disappeared, and then moved on. Sutton, swinging a mile off trail to their left, kept the horses at a walk in order to avoid stirring up a yellow pall of their own.

He rode in silence, conscious of the withering heat, eyelids pulled to narrow slits as he sought to minimize the desert's blinding glare, and wished the journey would end. It could, if the outlaws did as he expected and laid over in the Mexican settlement for the night.

When they drew near the town he again halted, choosing a deep, sandy draw that hid them from the settlement. Waiting there until almost dark, they finally resumed the ride. By then Jack reasoned, the outlaws would be feeling secure, having seen no evidence of further pursuit.

Carneros seemed to be a small village consisting of a dozen or so adobe huts, a church, and a group of larger buildings apparently having something to do with the government, all surrounded by a few impoverished looking farms. As they approached the first of these lying adjacent to the road, a man hoeing corn with a crude mattock paused, stared at them curiously. Sutton guided the bay to him.

"*Buenos días, señor,*" he greeted. "The day is a hot one."

The Mexican mopped at the sweat glistening on his swarthy face. "It is true."

"Two men rode this way. Do you know where they went?"

The farmer nodded. "I do. They ask a question: where is the house of Ascensión Chavez."

"Did you tell them this?"

"I did," the man said and leaned on his mattock expectantly.

Sutton reached into his pocket and procured a silver dollar. He flipped it to the man. "You will tell us this bit of information also, please."

The farmer pocketed the coin. "You must ride through the village to the headquarters of the *rurales*. It is the third house beyond it—one of a blue door with yellow roses growing in the yard."

"Gracias," Sutton said, and cut back to Gerlay's side. "He say something about the *rurales?*" the deputy asked immediately.

Jack grinned tightly. "Headquarters," he said, pointing at the cluster of buildings they had noted earlier. "Probably a *commandante* and a dozen or so men."

"Damn the lousy luck," Gerlay muttered. "We're fools to go busting in here."

"Nothing else we can do," Sutton replied. "Just ride easy."

They came to the structure occupied by the army, and passed by in wary silence. Undoubtedly the men were all inside seeking relief from the heat. A short distance farther, the house where the outlaws were said to have gone was instantly recognizable. Dismounting in the shadow of the hut behind it, they crossed to the rear of the Chavez place. Pausing, Jack studied the low, unplastered building. A door and a solitary window faced them from that angle. There were no signs of life.

Back in the center of the village children were playing, their voices riding clear on the hot stillness. Somewhere a donkey brayed. It was yet too early for the evening meal but smoke lifted from a few chimneys as housewives began their preparations.

"You figure they're in there?" Gerlay asked in a low voice. "Don't see no horses."

Jack pointed to a small, thatch-roofed shed to their left. "In there probably."

"Want me to take a look?"

"Not worth the risk; you'd be in full view of the house." He hesitated, then added, "We'll know soon enough."

Checking his pistol, he started for the door of Chavez's hut. Gerlay fell in beside him. Halfway Jack slowed, laid a restraining hand on the deputy's arm.

"Watch your shooting. . . ."

Ben Gerlay nodded. "Don't worry none about me."

The door of the Chavez house flew open. Two men leaped into the yard, guns raised. Sutton felt a bullet whip past his head, another tug at his sleeve. He hurled himself to the ground, realizing in that fragment of time that it had been a trap—that the outlaws had bribed the farmer to direct them.

Gerlay was firing back. Sutton saw Joe Harp stiffen from a crouch, spin half around and fall heavily. Jack threw a furious glance at the deputy and then aimed at Stinger Jones, leveling at the man's leg. In that same moment Gerlay got off a shot. The outlaw jumped as the bullet sliced across his forearm.

"Hold your fire!" Jack yelled at the deputy. And then swung his attention to Jones. "Stinger! Throw down your gun! I'm a U.S. Marshal—"

"The hell with you!" the outlaw shouted back and ducked into the open doorway. Half hidden, he lifted his pistol to fire point blank at Sutton.

Jack saw him aim, threw himself to one side, trying frantically to avoid the bullet. He had a quick glimpse of Ben Gerlay crouched a yard or so to his right, still shooting; he heard shouts coming from somewhere behind—and then darkness, like a vast, black cloud, descended upon him.

VI

Rough hands dragged Jack Sutton to his feet. Half conscious, he stood there in the semi-darkness, vaguely aware of others crowding about, of the close, stifling heat. He was in some sort of room. There were bars on the high, small windows.

"*Ándale! Ándale!*"

The same hands jerked him half around. Anger flamed through him and he struck out blindly, gasped with pain as someone drove a rifle butt savagely into his left kidney, sending him to his knees.

"*Gringo cabrono!*"

"For Christ's sake, Sutton—"

As from a great distance, he heard Ben Gerlay's strained voice as he struggled to his feet.

"Quit fighting 'em. . . . They'll kill us all."

Sutton's head began to clear. Ignoring waves of

nausea, he looked around. There were two other prisoners besides the deputy and himself. Both were Mexicans, one elderly, the other considerably younger. Two heavily armed guards in makeshift uniforms were prodding them toward an open door.

"*Ándale!*"

Jack stumbled as one of the soldiers gave him a shove. Cold fury gripped him and he wheeled, fists clenched. The guard raised his rifle threateningly. Sutton relented, moved on with the others into a small courtyard.

A third *rurale* stepped aside, drew open a second door in the opposite wall, and pulled himself to rigid attention. Jack, faculties now nearing normal, strode by him into a large room. A slim, dark eyed officer in a gaudy blue uniform piped with gold braid sat behind a desk. He looked more like a member of the *Federales,* or possibly the elite palace guard, than a *rurale.*

"The prisoners, my captain," the guard announced.

Sutton and the others were lined up before the officer who continued to laze in his chair as he idly watched the proceedings. When the shuffling had stilled, he sat up and squared his shoulders.

"I am Captain Juan Torrero," he said in Spanish, and then faced Sutton. "The language is understood?"

Sutton nodded. "What the hell's this all about?"

Torrero shifted his cool glance to Gerlay, ignoring the question. "And you?"

"I understand."

"Good. It will be much easier—"

Sutton took a half step forward and steadied himself, palms down on the desk. "I want an answer, *Commandante*—" he began, and then felt sickening pain surge through him once again as one of the guards applied the stock of his rifle. Fighting the nausea, Sutton's head dropped, but he held on grimly.

"Contain yourself," Torrero's smooth, liquid voice bit into his consciousness. "My men have short patience. In my court—"

"Court!" Sutton blurted the word. "What right have you got to drag us into court?"

"To answer the charge of murder," the officer replied quietly.

Sutton's jaw sagged. He pulled back from the desk, stared numbly at Torrero. The *commandante,* smiling ingratiatingly, turned his attention to the Mexican prisoners. His dark face grew stern.

"You are brothers of the name Bernal?"

"Yes, Excellency."

"You are accused of theft—an animal belonging to the hacienda of Emeterio Gomez. There is proof of the fact. You are therefore guilty."

"Yes, my captain, but it was a matter of food. My family starves, and the cow was old—sick."

"That is of no consideration. A crime has been committed. You are sentenced to five years."

The two men stood silent, stunned by such swift, ruthless justice. And then the younger of the two rushed forward. He was dressed, as his brother, in the loose white drawers and jumper favored by the peons with the exception of a bright red scarf worn about his waist as a belt.

"Five years!" he cried unbelievingly. "You cannot—"

The older Bernal pulled him back, faced the officer. "Please, Excellency—do not do this to Eduardo. He is young and had little to do with the theft. The fault was mine. Permit me to serve ten years and set him free."

"Hold them," Torrero ordered unfeelingly and motioned to one of the guards.

The Bernals were dragged from the room into the courtyard. Torrero fixed his bird-like attention on Sutton and Ben Gerlay.

"You are recovered from your wound, I trust?" he asked politely, smiling at Jack.

Wound . . . ? Sutton had forgotten it. Abruptly aware of a slight burning along the side of his head, he touched it gingerly. There was a soreness, and blood laid a dry crust across a narrow length where Stinger Jones' bullet had creased him. But there was a second tenderness. He felt of it, frowned.

Torrero said, "I regret the necessity for that. You resisted with great violence; my men were forced to subdue you."

Sutton stirred angrily. "Forget it!" he snarled. "I demand to know what this is all about!"

"It is not your privilege to demand," the officer replied smoothly. "You are not in the United States—you are in Mexico where you will answer to the charge of murder."

"Murder! Whose murder?" Ben Gerlay gasped.

"A countryman of yours of the name Harp."

Jack Sutton recoiled in surprise. After a moment he recovered, said, "It was not murder, Captain. He and his partner fired upon us first."

"Which of you loosed the bullet that killed the man?"

"How could I know that? We both were shooting."

Juan Torrero drummed thoughtfully upon his desk. He shook his head. "There is a variation. It was reported by a witness that the attack was forced by you. During such, the man Harp was murdered."

"That was not the way of it!" Sutton said, holding to his temper. "This witness—is he called by the name Jones?"

"That is the name."

"He's a goddam liar!" Gerlay shouted in English. "Bring him here and I'll make him tell it right—"

"Unfortunately that is not possible; important business awaited him elsewhere. But that is of no consequence. I have his report of the incident."

"A lie, Captain," Jack said. "And I think you know it."

Torrero leaned forward. "It is no lie that a man of the name Harp was slain by one of you. Such is fact, and upon that truth I must base the determination of guilt and punishment."

"We're American citizens," Gerlay said, still in English. "We're entitled to—"

"You are entitled to nothing except the justice of this court."

Disgust and frustration overwhelmed Jack Sutton. "Court—this is no court. It is a—"

"Have care!" Torrero warned. "I am the commander of this area. And as such I shall judge you as your courts judge my countrymen when they are accused of crimes north of the border!"

Sutton shook himself wearily. "This man you rely upon as a witness, he is an outlaw. We followed him and Harp because of a bank they robbed." He started to reveal that both he and Gerlay were lawmen, then thought better of it. In Torrero's mind it would have no bearing on the matter.

"Perhaps," the officer said, "but I see no importance to such a fact. A man was killed in this province. It is with that I am concerned."

"I have friends in El Paso," Jack said, grasping now at straws in a final effort to deter Torrero. "They may also be friends of yours. If permitted I will contact them. They will assure you that we are not criminals—that Harp and Jones are."

"Again I say such is not of importance. A crime is on trial here. And since it cannot be determined which of you fired the fatal bullet, both must pay the penalty. In this I have no choice."

A door in the far wall opened. A large, hard mouthed man with nose flattened and twisted askew, entered. He wore lace boots and black corded pants marked with dust and grease stains. His shirt was open down the front, displaying a sweaty mat of dark hair.

64

He nodded to Torrero and said, "The two prisoners are ready, Captain?"

"Four," the officer corrected.

The big man's eyes registered surprise. "Four? That is good." He gave Sutton and Gerlay a swift glance. "These?"

"They are the ones, Kollar. They have been found guilty of the crime of murder. I have sentenced them to ten years of labor."

Gerlay moaned. Shock numbed Jack Sutton. It was unbelievable—yet it was happening. He turned to Kollar.

"He's making a mistake. We're not guilty."

"Nobody ever is," the thick shouldered man said in an off-hand way and moved to Torrero's desk. "Who did they kill, Captain? One of your soldiers?"

"A man of the name Harp."

"A North American, eh?" Kollar squinted at Sutton. "Be damn glad it wasn't a Mexican," he said in English. "He'd a given you life for that."

"It was a fair fight," the deputy explained hurriedly. "Shoot-out. Just happened Harp caught a bullet. You're an American like us—make him understand!"

Kollar wagged his large head. "Not me. You won't catch me butting into the *commandante's* business. He says you're guilty—that's it."

Reaching into his pocket, Kollar drew forth a leather pouch. "How much, Captain?"

"One hundred American dollars each—gold."

Sutton stared at the officer and then at Kollar. "What

the hell's this?" he demanded in a hard voice.

Kollar opened his pouch, dumped a pile of gold pieces onto the desk. Methodically he counted out the prescribed amount.

Jack gripped the man by the arm. "What's this mean?"

Kollar shook free of Sutton's grasp. "Mean?" he said, starting to replace the remaining coins in the sack. "Means you and your friend there—and them two *peons*—belong to me—lock, stock and barrel. I own the lot of you."

"Slave labor," Gerlay muttered in a stricken voice.

"Kind of a hard way to put it, but you are going to be working in a silver mine, down near Santa Eulalia."

"You can't do this!" the deputy continued. "We're American citizens—"

"You ain't nothing," Kollar snapped, his manner changing. "Make up your mind to that. And I been doing it for years—Captain here and a couple more of his *compadres* keep me supplied with labor."

"It ain't nothing but pure slavery—"

Kollar shook his head. "Not that at all. You're criminals, sentenced to serve time. I just take you off the government's hands, save them the expense of feeding and keeping you. And I go by the rules: when a man's time is up, he goes his way."

Sutton listened in silence. "You won't get away with this for long. Authorities on the other side of the border will find out someday, step in . . ."

"Not much they won't. The old U.S.A. ain't going to

stick it's neck in Mexico's business. You committed a crime; you got tried and sentenced for it. That's what it amounts to. . . . Them others ready, Captain?"

Torrero motioned to one of the guards who disappeared into the courtyard and returned moments later with the Bernals. At the sight of Kollar, the elder brother halted abruptly.

"No!" he cried, his eyes spreading with terror. "The Mariposa!"

He turned, tried to bolt. The guard caught him by the arm, whirled him back, and sent him sprawling on the floor in front of Torrero's desk.

"Watch him," Kollar said, and stepping to the door, yelled an order. Immediately, two men appeared, each carrying a rifle and short lengths of chain at the ends of which were metal cuffs.

"Need a couple more sets," Kollar said. "Captain's got two more for us."

One of the men dropped his chains on the floor, wheeled, and went back into the yard.

Kollar kicked the manacles toward Jack and the deputy. "Put 'em on."

Gerlay remained motionless, staring at the irons. Kollar leaned forward, struck the deputy sharply on the side of the head with an open palm. Gerlay reeled and fell back against the wall. Dazed, he slid to a sitting position. Kollar nudged the chains closer to him with his toe.

"You hear? Put 'em on!"

The deputy began to fit the cuffs around his ankles.

The mining man swung his close attention to Sutton. "You too, bucko."

"The hell with you!" Jack yelled, anger exploding suddenly within him.

Crouched low, he lunged at Kollar, drove his knotted fist into the big man's expressionless face. Kollar staggered back. As Torrero yelled, Sutton smashed a second blow into Kollar's belly—and then the curtain of black riding a mountain of pain descended on him again.

VII

Sutton first became aware of a low, rumbling sound, and then a succession of hard jolts sent pain stabbing through his aching body, bringing him upright.

It was near sunset. He was in a wagon—an old, high-sided ore carrier that had been fitted out with benches. Ben Gerlay was next to him, face buried in his hands. The Bernal brothers sat opposite and were regarding him with close intent. Chains at his feet jingled and he looked down. The iron cuffs around his ankles brought instant realization, and impulsively, he started to rise.

"No, *señor*," the elder Bernal warned softly, and pointed to the two guards sitting at the end of the wagon.

Face grim, Sutton settled back. He glanced to the high seat beyond Gerlay. Kollar's broad shape was silhouetted against the darkening sky. He was leaning forward, elbows upon his knees, reins looping from his hands. They were crossing a broad flat.

"You took one hell of a beating," Gerlay said in a low voice.

Jack shifted on the hard plank. "Feel like it. How long we been on the move?"

"Hour—little more."

"You are a brave—but I think foolish—man," the older Bernal said. "I am called Celestino. My brother is Eduardo. You are of the name Jack Sutton; your friend and I have spoken together."

Jack nodded, acknowledging the introduction. "You know this place where we are being taken?"

Celestino sighed deeply. "The Mariposa, a terrible place. Better it should be called hell. The guards are animals—even worse. There is poor food, little water and long hours of the hardest labor."

"You have been there before?"

Celestino shook his head. "I only know the place by reputation. One who is sent there is not likely to return."

I'll return, Jack Sutton thought, staring off into oncoming darkness. *I've got to—I can't let Billy's time run out. I'll get that letter off to Henry Parmelee, ask for a delay—but he won't hold off indefinitely—and what real assurance can I give him that I will come back with Stinger Jones? I've got to start all over again—and God only knows where I'll find him—and when.*

Weighted by fatigue, senses dulled by monotonous aches and pain, Sutton dozed. Around midnight he awoke, his first thoughts on the possibility of escape. He glanced at Kollar, the mining man was still hunched on the seat, perhaps half asleep. Jack cast a covert look at the two guards; both were watching him with narrow interest.

After a few minutes he gave up the idea. Later an opportunity would present itself, or he would manufacture an opportunity, if necessary. Hampered by the leg irons, the bright moonlight, and under the watchful eyes of the guards, a break would be impossible. Later . . .

He slept again, roused near sunrise, and looked about. They had left the flat and entered a long, deep canyon. They were in the Sierra Madres, he realized somewhere along the east slope and not far from the northern tip of the vast range.

"We are not far," Celestino said, scanning the rocks and brush with a hopeless glance.

Ben Gerlay and Eduardo awoke. The younger Bernal surveyed the seared land to either side.

"It is not a place where one would hold a fiesta," he observed with dry humor.

Celestino shrugged. "It is clear you do not know well our destination, otherwise you would not treat the matter so lightly."

"A face of gloom will not change things," Eduardo

replied. "Who knows? Perhaps there can be an escape."

"There has never been an escape. Such is hopeless."

The sun came out and it was hot immediately. The tortured country about them seemed to recoil, prepare itself for the burning onslaught. They followed along the floor of the canyon, the iron-shod wheels of the wagon stirring up boils of choking, yellow dust as they cut into narrow ruts and jolted over half buried rocks. An hour later they swung off abruptly onto a side road.

Instantly, like silent shadows, half a dozen Yaqui Indians rose from the stunted brush and glistening, heat cracked rocks. They stared with dark, expressionless faces at the wagon and those aboard as it climbed slowly up the slope.

Kollar came to life, turned his head and grinned at Sutton. There was a dark welt on his face where Jack's fist had caught him.

"Them's my pet watchdogs," he said. "They're the boys who'll drag you back if you're damn fool enough to escape. They ain't lost a man for me yet."

Sutton was giving little thought to the Yaquis visible; he was looking beyond them, wondering if there were others scattered along the base of the mountain. He could see none, and decided there was but the one group. The slope appeared to be a series of ledges and bluffs that would make descent impossible, except by the road which had been blasted and hewn from the rock.

"Something else you ought to know," Kollar continued. "They don't mind how they bring you back. Sort of favor a rope, howsomever—with them doing the dragging."

Sutton made no reply. Kollar was endeavoring to get a rise out of him but he would not accept the bait. Better assume an air of resignation and hopelessness. It could improve chances for escape later.

"Up there," Celestino murmured, pointing toward the summit of the mountain with his chin.

Sutton shifted his gaze. The road terminated on a narrow plain where a row of adobe huts and several individual buildings stood in the glaring sunlight. A few men wearing wide brimmed hats and armed with pistols and clubs moved indolently about. At the lower end of the small flat two dozen men, stripped to the waist, were loading ore into a string of large wagons.

Higher on the barren slope above the plain, a dark hole marked the entrance to the mine. Broken rock and baked earth scarred the area below it. As Jack watched, two men appeared in the entrance to the shaft. They moved slowly out into the sunlight, bent forward, as they pulled a small four-wheeled cart. A third man pushed. Traveling at snail's pace, they came into the open, crossed a narrow level, and began the descent to the stockpile at the end of the plain.

Celestino Bernal cried softly. "It is Reyes Villar who pushes!"

Sutton stared at the emaciated, ragged man laboring at the rear of the cart. "A friend?"

"Yes. One of long duration. A year past he disappeared. We thought him dead."

Gerlay swore. Jack said, "Why does your government permit this?"

"They are unaware," Celestino replied. "It is true there are prison farms and certain industries where convict labor is used, but they know nothing of such arrangements as this. It exists between the mining companies of ill repute and men of Torrero's nature."

The wagon jolted across the plain, passing the line of huts, and halted before the largest of the remaining buildings. Kollar rose stiffly to his feet.

"Morales!" he shouted.

Immediately a squat, thick shouldered Mexican came through the doorway and paused, hands on hips, in the harsh sunshine. Sweat glistened on his face, soaked the armpits of his faded shirt, and laid dust-covered streaks down the legs of his cotton pants. He surveyed the prisoners in the wagon, then grinned at Kollar.

"Four, eh? The fishing was good."

Kollar brushed at his eyes. "Couple of Americanos."

"Too bad," Morales said shrugging. "The gringos do not last long."

"These are tough ones," Kollar answered, looking directly at Sutton. "That one I have business with another time when it is not so hot."

Morales studied the bluish swelling on the mining man's cheek, but carefully avoided comment. "He is trouble, eh?"

"Not as much as he will get. Warn Parado."

A slow, expectant smile had spread across Morales' features. He reached back inside the hut to pick up a whip that lay on a table.

"None are so tough they cannot be tamed," he said and moved toward the wagon. He stopped a few paces beyond and beckoned imperiously. "Come!"

The Bernals, carrying the chains that linked their ankles, climbed from the vehicle. Sutton and Gerlay followed. Morales circled them, eyeing each man critically.

"Remove the irons," he directed.

The guard procured a key from his pocket, and knelt to unlock the cuffs. After a few moments he stepped back, dragging the chains with him.

"To the tunnel," Morales said, and pointed up the slope with his whip.

Sutton and the others turned and began to ascend the slight grade. Suddenly a sharp crack broke the heated silence. Celestino Bernal screamed with pain, clawing at his buttocks. Quick rage boiled through Jack Sutton. He halted in his tracks and braced himself for the lash of the whip, not certain he could control himself when the blow came.

"Go!" Morales shouted, and laughed.

They moved on. From his place on the wagon Kollar said, "Put them in Number Six with Garcia."

"Number Six," Morales echoed.

Bitterness a sullen current within him, Sutton marched with the others up the slope and into the mine's entrance. Another guard appeared in the dust that hung, like a thin curtain, in the stale, hot air.

"Halt!" Morales shouted, and popped his whip above the head of Celestino Bernal. The old man flinched, but uttered no sound.

"New workers," Morales said, coiling his whip. "The big gringo is a bad one. Watch him well."

Parado was lean, muscular. He nodded slowly. "This I shall do.

He remained unmoving until Morales had turned and gone back into the open. Evidently Morales was the yard overseer while Parado had charge of the men inside the mine. After a moment he stepped closer and looked each man over carefully, as had Morales.

He started to speak, but hesitated as the grating sound of wheels came from the tunnel behind him. Moving aside, he motioned for Sutton and the others to do likewise. A moment later one of the ore carts, drawn by two hollow-eyed men and pushed by a third, emerged from the pall.

"The dead who walk," Eduardo muttered.

Instantly Parado lifted his whip, sent it streaking toward the younger Bernal. It cracked viciously only inches above the boy's head.

"Silence! You are forbidden to speak!"

The wagon rolled by, and disappeared gradually into the murk. The overseer faced them.

"I am Luis Parado. You will do well to heed my words. You will work. There will be no talking. If you wish water or desire to relieve yourself you will first ask my permission. In all matters you will come to me. Am I understood?"

Celestino nodded woodenly. Eduardo stirred and Ben Gerlay shrugged. Sutton only stood in sullen silence. Immediately Parado's hand tightened about the handle of his whip.

"Speak, gringo. Am I understood?"

Jack moved his head grudgingly.

Parado fell back, his hard eyes on Sutton. "You will do well to answer when spoken to. The tip of my whip is of silver. It cuts deep."

Sutton could contain his anger no longer. "You touch me with that—I'll kill you!"

The overseer's lids narrowed. "Do not speak of killing, gringo; it is not a thought that will bring you profit. We have ways of dealing with the defiant." Coiling his whip, he tucked it under his arm, then said, "Proceed into the tunnel."

They moved deeper into the mine, walking slowly through the choking dust. Sounds of digging reached them: the measured *chunk-chunk* of striking picks, the harsh scrape of shovels scooping up ore, and the dull thud as it was tossed into carts. The dust thinned as they passed under an air shaft and it was a little cooler. Lanterns hung from the shoring at variable distances and other guards were encountered along the way.

Finally they broke out into a fairly large chamber where two dozen or so men labored to fill waiting carts. Parado beckoned to one of the four guards stationed in the room.

76

"New workers," he said, and then, pointing at Jack, added, "if this one opposes you, notify me."

The man nodded. He reached forth, put his broad hand upon the shoulder of Celestino, and shoved him toward the prisoners who were digging.

"Find yourself a pick, old man. Hurry!"

Eduardo started to follow his brother. The guard seized him by the arm, swung him against one of the carts. "No, rooster, you will find a shovel that fits you well. And work fast. The stockpile is low."

The younger Bernal lowered his head and, bending down, picked up a scoop and joined the others mechanically filling one of the wagons.

The guard then turned to Sutton and Gerlay. He looked them up and down, smiled with satisfaction. "You are strong ones. There will be no need for a pusher."

"I am no burro—" Ben Gerlay blurted unthinkingly.

The guard straightened, lifted his club. Parado, in the act of lighting a cigarette, paused.

"There is an objection?" the guard asked softly.

Gerlay subsided, shaking his head in a helpless way.

"Good," the man said. He glanced to the first wagon. "The load is ready. Take up the tongue. You will be directed as to where it must go."

Parado wheeled and started back into the tunnel as Sutton and the deputy moved to the front of the cart. The short tongue had been fitted with a crosspiece against which each man placed his chest.

"Go—gringo burros!" the guard laughed and struck

77

the side of the wagon with his club.

Gerlay cursed, threw his weight forward. Sutton, again fighting his temper, heaved with him. The cart began to roll, and they got under way, heading into the dust-bound shaft.

The day, filled with endless, monotonous journeys back and forth, ended with sundown. Aching, bone tired, Sutton and Gerlay were herded into the open with the other prisoners and marched down onto the level where the huts stood. They were taken then to a building somewhat apart from the rest where a number of wooden tubs, filled with water, were arranged on low benches. Five minutes were allowed for the men to wash away the sweat and dust accumulated during the day.

Jack Sutton, smoldering under the degrading, backbreaking labor stripped to his shirt and glanced about. Most of the men were too weak to take advantage of the cooling water. Gaunt scarecrows, they merely squatted against the side of the building, waiting in hopeless silence.

Few words had passed between Sutton and Gerlay during the interminable hours since their arrival. For one thing, there was little opportunity as the guards were always nearby and brooked no infraction of the no-talking rule. But mostly Jack Sutton's mind was occupied with thoughts of escape; it must be effected as soon as possible.

By noon of that day he had established the lay-out of the Mariposa firmly in mind; what lay beyond the plain was a different matter, however—one he had yet to determine. He hoped the Bernals could supply him with the needed information; failing there, he would manage, somehow, to question one of the other prisoners.

Gerlay, face haggard and drawn, mopped at his face with his shirt, looked off into the camp. "What comes next?" he wondered in a dispirited voice.

"It is the time for eating," a man beside him at the tub replied in good English.

"No talking!" a guard nearby shouted and moved instantly toward the speaker.

The Mexican straightened up. There were scars on his back and he was thin to the point of emaciation, but his eyes held a hard, glittering depth in which there was no fear. The guard stared at him for a long minute, then turning, deliberately spat, and sauntered back to his position, swaggering slightly to cover his embarrassment.

Jack studied the Mexican with interest. Here was one man Kollar and his *brutos* had not broken. He would be a good one to know.

A whistle shrilled through the hush. The prisoners assembled, forming a line, and started across the clearing toward an elongated, low roofed building erected crosswise at the end of the plain. It had small, high placed windows and a single door at which guards stood on either side.

The men filed in silently and took positions at the long tables crowding the room. It was almost as hot within the structure as it had been outside in the direct sun. The heat, Jack saw, was originating in the kitchen, an area partitioned off at one end.

Two prisoners served as trusties. They brought in the meal—a shallow plate of thin corn cakes heavily larded with chili over which hot grease had been poured. Watery, lukewarm chocolate was provided as a beverage.

Jack's stomach refused the greasy mess and he contented himself with only the chocolate. The remainder of the prisoners ate greedily, cleaning their plates with care. When the meal was finished, Sutton heard a step behind him. He looked up to see Kollar.

"What's the matter, bucko—you don't eat?"

"Not fit for hogs," Sutton replied flatly.

Kollar stiffened. Two guards stepped to his side quickly, their clubs ready. The mining man remained silent for several moments, and then he waved them back.

"It is not necessary," he said in Spanish, and then in English to Jack: "You and me's got a little date one of these evenings. I'll let you know when."

"Any time," Sutton replied quietly.

Kollar grinned and walked away. The whistle shrilled again. The prisoners rose, turned to the door and marched into the open. Halting, they formed a ragged line. Morales and Parado appeared, and walked the length of the formation, scrutinizing each man much as a military officer inspects his troops.

But it was for different purpose. When they reached

the end of the line, Parado said, "The count is correct: thirty-four."

Morales nodded, stood by idly smacking the palm of his hand with the butt of his whip. *"Recreación!"* he shouted abruptly, and turning on his heel, strode toward one of the lesser buildings.

The line broke. Men began to move off into the open yard, now darkening as sunlight faded. Sutton glanced around. Apparently it was a free time period granted the prisoners during which they could relax—if possible—and attend to personal needs. Two or three wandered back toward the tubs evidently to again soak up some of the moisture their dehydrated bodies craved. Others moved for the latrines, but most sank onto the still warm sand, too exhausted to indulge in wasted motion.

Jack studied the yard. Guards were posted at various points, forming an irregular circle. No one, presumably, could go beyond the imaginary line their positions established. With Gerlay and the Bernals, he crossed the compound slowly, taking note of all things that might be of future use. No words passed between the men as the rule of silence was still in effect.

Shortly before dark, Parado's whistle once more broke the quiet. The men shambled wearily into line, as before. Kollar and Morales came from their quarters, and stood in the open doorway smoking slim, black cigars.

Luis Parado faced the prisoners. "Number One!" he shouted.

Six men pulled out of the irregular formation, headed for the hut at the end of the row. Two guards waited at the door. When the prisoners had entered, the heavy panel was slammed shut and a thick crossbar was dropped into place, securing it.

"Number Two!"

A like procedure was followed for all the remaining men. Sutton, Gerlay and the Bernals were assigned to hut Number Six. It only had one occupant—the lean, hard-eyed Mexican who had faced down the guard at the tubs.

He led the way into the small, cell-like room. It was lined on two sides with tiers of three bunks, and it was rancid with the sickening odor of filthy bedding, urine, and hot; stale air. When the door closed and a thud announced the dropping of the bar into its iron brackets, the Mexican wheeled to his new cellmates. His lips were drawn into a tight smile.

"Now we speak—the *bastardos* cannot hear if the voice is low. I am Miguel Garcia. Tonight I will escape this hell—or I will die."

VIII

A STARTLED SILENCE GRIPPED THE ROOM. SOMEWHERE along the row of huts a man was coughing in deep, hacking gasps, that tormented sound mingling with the measured beat of a horse moving down the road.

Gerlay found his voice. "Take us with you, friend," he said in a hurried way, and then, casting a glance at Sutton, added, "That right, Marshal?"

Jack frowned. He was anxious to escape the Mariposa—it was imperative, in fact, but failure would be fatal. "What of the Yaquis?"

"It is impossible," Celestino Bernal said heavily, sinking onto one of the lower bunks. "It is said no man escapes this place. . . . I so believe."

"It is said!" Garcia echoed scornfully. "I will escape—"

"Or you will die. That is more likely."

"I will escape," Garcia insisted stubbornly. "See—already I have taken the first steps."

He moved to the back wall and dropped to his knees. Clawing about in the loose dust he uncovered a well-worn table knife. Holding it aloft, he said, "This I managed when a mistake was made in the dining quarters. It fell to the floor unnoticed; I recovered it."

Turning swiftly, he began to dig at the mortar locking the adobe bricks in the wall. It was no more than a thin crust and came away easily, freeing a number of the mud blocks.

"Each night I have dug until almost time for the day, Then, with urine, I would mix mortar and seal over the work accomplished. Now all is ready. Enough adobes can be removed to permit the passage of a man's body."

"It is of little use," Celestino said, settling back on the hard bed.

83

Miguel glanced to Sutton. Jack shrugged, said, "He is right. How will you get from the mountain? Have you for gotten the Yaquis?"

"They must be avoided," Garcia admitted thoughtfully "Today you passed that way. Were there many?"

"I counted eight on the road—more could have been in the brush. It makes little difference—a man cannot get off the mountain without passing them. The bluffs are twenty, perhaps thirty meters high." Jack shook his head. "Do not be a fool, Miguel."

"But I must escape. It is of importance—"

"It is of importance to me, also. If I fail, my brother will die for something he did not do."

"Maybe it's worth the chance," Gerlay said in English. "Five of us. If we all go at once could be we'd be able to handle the Yaquis."

"With one worn-out table knife between us? You know better than that, Ben," Jack said. He looked at Garcia. "A good plan is needed."

Eduardo Bernal's face showed interest for the first time. It was apparent he was willing to place his hope and trust in Sutton. Pulling the scarf he employed as a belt tighter, he hunched against the wall.

"You have a plan?"

Jack shrugged, crossed to the rear of the hut. There was no window, only a small port near the roof through which air could enter.

"What is beyond the mountain?"

"A long trail of much difficulty, after which comes the desert of Sonora," Celestino replied.

"Nogales would be the first town of size?"

"Three hundred kilometers, more or less. And do not forget the Yaquis—somewhere between they would lie and wait."

Sutton nodded. "Is there water north of here?"

Bernal sucked at his lower lip. "It is only a guess. There are springs near the hills, but they could be dry this time of year. Once the hills are behind you, there is only the desert—the Chihuahua."

"Water can be carried," Gerlay remarked.

"I do not wish to go north," Miguel Garcia broke in petulantly. "My home is to the south—the city of Durango."

"A place of considerable distance," Celestino said. "How is it you were sent here?"

Garcia lifted his hands, allowed them to fall. "In my state I was a citizen of political importance. There was a disagreement among certain officials and myself. A charge was made and I was found guilty, although—before the Holy Virgin—I am innocent. I was sent to a prison in Durango, and then one day I was removed to this abode of vermin."

Garcia paused. Suddenly he plunged the knife he held into the loose sand. Eyes blazing, he faced the others. "It shall not always be like this! I will return to Durango—and there are those who shall pay!"

"I also have scores to settle," Gerlay murmured. "A popinjay officer in Carneros, a man named Jones . . ."

Sutton wheeled to the deputy. Ignoring Spanish, he rasped: "You don't touch Stinger Jones. He's my pris-

85

oner. . . . Remember that, Ben!"

"Have care!" Bernal hissed warningly. "The guards will hear—come."

Gerlay leaned back against the bunks. "Sure, Marshal. Mite hard to forget what he done to us. Expect first thing we'd better do, however, is figure a way out of here."

Jack looked down. His temper, Billy, the Mariposa—all were getting to him. He turned to Garcia.

"Do not try an escape tonight. You have made a beginning but more consideration must be given to such a dangerous effort. Delay for two, perhaps three days while the matter is thought out."

"I can see no good reason—"

"There is a truth you must face, Miguel. Escape cannot be made except by the road. That means also that the Yaquis must be passed. That is the heart of any plan—how to get by the Yaquis unseen. If such a miracle can be performed, and we are prepared for the desert, we then have a chance."

The elder Bernal bobbed his head. "Well spoken— and it is so. But there lies the impossibility. The Indians see and hear everything. Because of this the camp is but lightly guarded, as you have all noticed."

Jack shifted his attention back to Garcia. "You are agreeable to delay?"

Miguel toyed with a handful of sand, sifting it between his fingers. "I have waited too long now, months. . . . I will not remain much longer. Three days—no more." He reached for the knife, pulled it free and fell to examining its blunted point. "I have your word of honor that an escape will be made?"

Jack studied Garcia. It came to him suddenly that Miguel was slightly addled, that prison life—the terrible, exhausting labor in the Mariposa mine—had unhinged his mind to some extent. It was not hard to understand: between the grueling heat, the endless hours, poor food and brutal guards, the breaking point could soon be reached.

"You have my word," Sutton said quietly. "Meanwhile, use care. Avoid trouble. Should a guard become suspicious, all could be lost."

The next day was little different from the first. The prisoners were turned out at the crack of dawn, given a meal of watery corn mush and thin chocolate, and with the exception of those on punishment detail, were herded into the mine.

Sutton and Gerlay were again assigned to one of the carts. It was pure labor but it was considerably better than being one of those forced to load the big ore wagons. This was done at the stockpile—the point where the carts were emptied at the edge of the plain.

Prisoners worked stripped to the waist in the blazing sun throughout the day, scooping ore from the piles and tossing it into the much larger ore wagons. Only when there was no ore available were they permitted to seek out the thin shade and rest. Thus there was constant pressure on the men inside the mine to keep the carts filled, while the pullers and pushers of the small vehicles, as they were termed, were constantly prodded by the guards to deliver their loads faster.

On the third day Ben Gerlay was knocked to the ground for making a remark to one of the guards. He was not seriously injured but Jack feared the deputy would be sentenced to the yard crew, and redoubled his efforts to come up with a feasible escape plan. He could think of nothing and he began to fear that the monotonous, animal-like existence he was being compelled to lead was dulling his brain, turning him slowly but surely into one of the walking dead.

That night, after the brief recreation period was over and they were again locked in their stench-filled cell, Garcia cornered him.

"What of the escape? Are you not ready?"

Jack shrugged helplessly. "I have thought of nothing."

"Such planning takes time, Miguel," Celestino said gently. "Our lives will depend upon all matters going as they should."

"I cannot wait!" Garcia cried, moving about distractedly. "Too long now have I delayed."

The steady lope of a horse on the road came to them from the closing night. Sutton lifted his hand for silence. Gradually the hoof beats faded.

"Who is it that rides out each evening?" he asked.

Garcia shrugged. "Luis Parado. He has a great longing for the *putas* in the village of Antonito, south of here. Each night he pays them a visit."

Gerlay looked sharply at Jack. "Got an idea?"

"He is known to the Yaquis," Sutton said thoughtfully, not answering the deputy's question. "His passage likely is not noted."

"Not much help to us—only one horse."

"Probably be our only chance. As far as horses are concerned, you can forget them. If we get out of here it will be on foot."

The deputy groaned. Eduardo Bernal smiled wanly, then said, "To escape this place I would cross the Chihuahua on hands and knees."

"What is the plan?" Miguel Garcia asked, his dark features strained. "This I must know if I am to make a decision."

Jack considered the Mexican. It had occurred to him earlier that Garcia could not be all he professed, that he might actually be a plant put among them by Luis Parado, or possibly even Kollar to spy on them. He had decided earlier that Garcia was on the level, but now he felt his conviction weaken and concluded it was only prudent to take no chances.

"I have a plan," he said, "but it is not complete. There are details to untangle. Tomorrow, or perhaps the next day, you shall know."

"An attempt will then be made?" Eduardo pressed eagerly.

"Let us say two nights from now, if all goes well." He looked at Garcia. "That is satisfactory?"

Miguel was silent for a time. Finally, "It is agreeable. What is there we must do?"

"Nothing. Do not speak of it, even among yourselves. Continue to avoid trouble. All else I shall handle."

"It is good," Celestino Bernal said, climbing into his bunk stiffly. "This night I shall sleep knowing there is hope."

Jack considered him with a half smile. "Pray a little for us, old one," he said. "It will not be easy."

The day passed slowly, as did all others—breathlessly hot, and filled with back-breaking toil. Two of the other prisoners collapsed while digging, and were dragged to the tubs where quantities of water were dumped on them until they revived. A rumor made the rounds that one of the men on punishment detail went berserk and killed a guard with a shovel. He was caught, but cheated the whip by dying.

Jack Sutton had his plan for escape fully formulated by dark. It was his intention to make the attempt that very night and not delay, as he had informed the others. Such was a precaution against the faint possibility of Miguel Garcia being a traitor.

When they were again locked in their cell, he moved immediately to the back wall and began to remove the loose adobes. Instantly his cellmates crowded around.

"We going tonight?" Gerlay asked, dropping beside him.

"Tonight," Jack said. "Get your knife, Miguel."

A low cry broke from Garcia's lips. He squatted, hurriedly dug up the blade.

"There is need to hurry," Sutton said, passing the bricks to the Bernals, also crouched around him. "We must be on the road before Parado."

The last of the adobes was removed. Listening briefly, Jack crawled through the opening. Cautioning the others to wait, he crawled to the front of the hut and looked into the yard. No one was in sight. The guards were gathered in one of the larger buildings, drinking and playing some sort of card game.

He returned to the rear of the hut. "Come," he whispered in an urgent voice.

Gerlay came through first, followed by Garcia, Eduardo and then Celestino. Sutton beckoned them in close.

"Quiet," he murmured. "The Yaquis may be near."

Turning, he moved off through the still warm rocks and dust-covered brush toward the road. They were ahead of Parado, he knew; all that remained now was to locate a place along the confined, twisting route where the overseer could be intercepted. It should be far enough from the camp for sounds to go unheard in the event Parado raised an outcry—yet a safe distance from the Yaqui camp.

He had considered the possibility of Parado not making his usual visit to the village that night; it seemed unlikely, but if it occurred, he would have to convince his friends, particularly Miguel Garcia, that the wisest thing to do was return and try again the following night. The others would listen, he was certain, but he was not so sure of Garcia.

They gained the road and moved silently along the shoulder. A sharp bend appeared, overhung by crowding boulders. Sutton halted.

"Here is the place," he said. "Celestino, you and your brother, with Miguel, will stand on the opposite side. Keep well hidden in the brush. Gerlay and I'll remain here. When Parado comes by, I will leap upon him from the rocks. Eduardo, it is then your job to capture the horse while we silence the man. Do it quickly as he must not run away."

"What about me?" the deputy asked.

"You're behind me. If I miss, you jump—one of us is bound to take him off the saddle. Main thing is to keep it all quiet—and don't let him yell."

"For me there is nothing to be done?" Garcia wondered, his tone injured.

"A great deal. Remove your clothing. You will wear that of Parado—if all goes well."

Gerlay shook his head. "Still like to know what we're planning—"

"He comes," Eduardo cut in quietly.

Sutton raised his hand for silence. The beat of the guard's horse was a soft, muted thud in the dust. "Your places," he whispered, and climbed to a high point on the rocky shoulder.

In only moments Luis Parado rode into view. He was slumped in the saddle, hat pushed to the back of his head. The reins were looped over the huge horn of his ornate Mexican saddle while he gave his attention to a bottle of wine he carried.

Jack waited until the man was directly below and then launched himself from the overhang. He caught the overseer around the arms, pinning them tightly, and both went off the startled horse in a writhing embrace.

They struck the ground with jarring force, Parado on the bottom, bearing the brunt of the impact. Jack was aware of the others swarming in, of the sudden tatoo of the horse's hoofs as he shied to one side, and then Luis Parado went limp in his grasp. He pulled back, saw Miguel Garcia crouched at his elbow, knife poised for a second blow while blood gushed from the overseer's throat.

Chilled by the callousness of the killing, Sutton got to his feet. He looked closely at Miguel's face; the man's eyes were bright and a satisfied smile pulled his lips tight across his teeth. Jack turned to see about the horse. Eduardo was holding him in a small pocket of brush off the road.

"That's done," Ben Gerlay said at his shoulder. "Garcia's pulling on Parado's duds. What's next?"

Sutton explained in Spanish. "Miguel will ride on, and try to pass himself by the Yaquis as Parado. They are much the same appearance."

"How will that help us?" the deputy asked.

"You will keep riding," Jack continued, now directing his words to Garcia. "You will be as Parado on his way to the village. After you leave the Indians, continue for five minutes, then return in a great hurry to them. Tell them you saw prisoners on the side of the mountain escaping."

Miguel nodded his understanding. "I take them with

me to this place, a distance from the road. While they are thus following, you will be able to escape."

"Yes. Once that is accomplished, you must continue on to the south. On the horse you can travel far before the escape is discovered."

"What of you? You will be on foot."

"Hiding will be simple in the brush along the mountain. For you there will be only open desert."

Gerlay shook his head, motioned at Garcia. "How do you know he'll come back once he gets by the Yaquis? He could keep going—not take any chances on his own neck."

Jack shrugged. There were no longer any doubts in his mind as to Miguel Garcia's sincerity; the lifeless body of Luis Parado proved that.

"I shall come back," Garcia said, crossing to where Eduardo held the horse. "It is a matter of honor."

He swung to the saddle with the easy grace of a natural rider, and pulled into the center of the road.

"Follow and listen with care," he said. "I shall whistle a song of my country. If you cease to hear, it will be a signal of danger."

"Understood," Sutton said. "Good luck."

"And to you good luck," Garcia said. "It is possible we will never meet again. Go with God."

IX

"*Vaya con Dios,*" murmured Celestino Bernal as Garcia faded into the pale darkness.

Jack Sutton turned an ear toward the camp. All was quiet. The sound of Garcia's whistling then reached him and he swung back, motioning to the others.

"Keep well in the shadows."

They struck off at once, Sutton and Ben Gerlay on one side of the road, the Bernals on the opposite. Fifty yards or so ahead Miguel Garcia rode slowly, his cheerful tune the solitary break in the warm hush.

A quarter of an hour later the whistling broke off. Jack halted, stopping the Bernals and the deputy. Garcia had probably reached the Indian camp and was passing by it at that very moment.

"Wait," he whispered and eased forward silently through the brush and rocks. Moments later he caught the reflected glow of a campfire against a stone slab. Pausing, he made careful inspection of the shadows and pockets of darkness nearby. Finally convinced that no one was close, he continued on. A dozen paces later he saw the camp.

He dropped low, hunched behind a clump of brittle-bush. Half a dozen Yaquis were gathered in the road, some standing, some squatting. Two more stood near the fire. Miguel Garcia had not halted, but was allowing his horse to proceed at a slow walk as he passed greetings to the Indians.

Some of the hard tension gripping Sutton faded. Miguel was getting away with the deception. He waited until the Mexican had disappeared into the void down the road, and the Yaquis had returned to their fire; then he retraced his steps to where Gerlay and the Bernals were waiting.

"Miguel is by them," he said when they gathered around. "We will move in. We will have but little time when he returns."

"How many Yaquis?" Celestino wanted to know.

"Counted eight."

"There could be more?" Gerlay said.

"Possibly. They were having their meal."

"One piece of luck," the deputy muttered. "We could have come when they were scattered all over the mountain."

"They still may be," Sutton said and moved off into the brush. "I couldn't see too good."

The deputy and the Bernals fell in behind him and they pushed on until they reached the point where Sutton had originally halted. The Yaquis were gathered around the fire, eating from a pot hanging over the flames. They ate greedily, reaching into the blackened container for steaming chunks of meat over which they smacked their lips noisily, licked their fingers and occasionally paused to wipe greasy drippings from their chins. Jack counted again. There were eleven.

"Where's Garcia?" the deputy muttered nervously. "Ought've been back by now. Still, it wouldn't surprise me none if he kept going."

Celestino Bernal interpreted the English correctly, and said, "He will return. He has given his word."

"His word! What is so important—"

The sudden hammer of a horse, running hard, checked Gerlay's voice. The Indians leaped to their feet, whirled to face the sound. A moment later Miguel Garcia burst into the flare of the fire's light. He pointed to the south, cried something in rapid Spanish, and then wheeling, rushed back down the road.

The Yaquis followed immediately, several pausing long enough to snatch up coils of rope. Sutton stalled a full minute and then, keeping to the edge of the rutted tracks, broke into a run.

They reached the Indian camp—no more than a clearing with a fire in the center—in a tight group. Jack moved toward the opposite side, his eyes on several skins of water hanging from a low cedar. They would never get across the Chihuahua Desert without a supply, and here was the means made to order. Behind him Celestino and Eduardo were fishing chunks of meat from the kettle, wrapping them in a bit of cloth they had found.

Sutton's hands closed around the rawhide strings tied to two of the water bags—actually a section of horse intestine, cleaned and closed at the ends. He saw motion to his left and spun. A Yaqui rose from the darkness beyond the ring of light. Apparently he had been sleeping when Garcia raised the alarm, or had been out of the camp for some reason.

The Indian's eyes spread in surprise. He looked wildly about and as Sutton lunged for his throat, he yelled. *"Aqui! Aqui! Prision—"*

Jack's throttling fingers shut off the rest of the word and they both went down in a thrashing heap. The Indian clawed at his eyes. He jerked aside, tightening his grip on the man's muscular throat. With his free hand he struck hard at the Indian's jaw. The Yaqui managed to turn his head, spoiling the blow. Metal glittered in his hand. Sutton grabbed frantically for the knife and felt the keen edge slice lightly across his palm.

He caught the man's wrist and forced it back, all the while increasing pressure on the windpipe. The Indian began to weaken. He struggled feebly, twisting his head from side to side, gasping for breath. Abruptly his body went lax.

Sutton picked up the knife and staggered to his feet. Gerlay and the Bernals were just behind him. Heaving for breath, he stared at them.

"Got—to run." he said hoarsely. "Somebody could—have heard."

Celestino nodded, thrust a water bag into his hands, and wheeled off into the brush at a trot. The deputy followed immediately but Eduardo paused, looked questioningly at Sutton.

"Go on!" Jack ordered impatiently. "I'll—keep up."

For a full hour Bernal maintained a steady pace, following an indefinite trail that laid its course across the slope of the mountain a dozen yards or so above the base. Finally, with all retching for breath, he halted.

"We rest," he said, and sank onto a ledge of rock.

The others sprawled out nearby. Sutton lay back and stared at the sky through overhanging brush. His throat was dry as gunpowder and it seemed impossible to suck enough air into his heaving lungs; his muscles ached with dull insistence.

"Reckon they're onto us yet?" Ben Gerlay asked. He no longer troubled to speak in Spanish as a courtesy to the Bernals, but simply addressed his remarks to Sutton.

"There has been time enough," Jack replied.

"Could be tracking us right now."

Celestino nodded. "They will come . . . soon."

Sutton turned to the older man. "How long?"

"One hour, perhaps less."

Jack drew himself upright. His breathing had returned to normal but the hard run had brought him almost to the point of exhaustion. The others were no better off, he realized.

"It is best we move on," he said. "The Yaquis will come very fast.

Celestino arose. "It is also wise to separate," he said in his calm, polite way. "A small trail is more easily hidden." Jack frowned. "Where will you go?"

"To relatives on the Sonora side of the Sierras. There we shall be safe. . . . Is it still in your mind to return to Carneros?"

"Such is necessary. The man I seek was last seen there. Also Torrero has our horses and guns."

"It is likely the Yaquis will search there, too."

"A chance we must take."

Celestino wagged his gray head doubtfully. "This one you seek, it must be a matter of importance, for it is a high price you will pay if caught."

"The importance concerns the life of my brother."

Celestino glanced at Eduardo. "I understand," he said. He touched his skin of water. "You have sufficient water?"

Sutton checked his bag, glanced at the one carried by the deputy. "Enough."

Eduardo removed the red sash he wore, and spread it on the dry ground. Unwrapping the cloth in which he carried the meat taken from the Yaqui camp, he divided the chunks equally. Keeping the bright colored sash, he passed the other packet to Gerlay.

"Eat well," he said, grinning broadly.

"We will leave you here," Celestino said when that was done. "Our trail climbs the mountain. You know the way to Carneros?"

"Due north—"

"It is possible to pass by the village if a course of exact north is maintained. Here is a way more simple: continue as we now go, along the foot of the mountain. By tomorrow late you will reach a small river that comes to you from the right hand. It is the Carretas.

"Perhaps there will be no water as there has been

100

little rain this year. Nevertheless, you will know it. If you will follow its course it will lead you to Carneros. Now, it is best we depart."

They shook hands all around solemnly, and the Bernals turned away, heading directly up the slope. Sutton and Gerlay moved on. They had the kinder trail; the Sierras were a rugged, towering range, reaching up to a twelve thousand feet altitude in some areas. To climb over the gigantic mass would be a difficult, slow task.

"You figure Garcia got away?" the deputy asked as he and Jack strode on through the night.

Sutton had pondered the question earlier. "Expect he did. That horse was a big advantage."

"Give my right arm to be in the saddle myself," Gerlay mumbled. "These goddam boots sure weren't made for walking."

Near dawn they paused, so worn they could go no farther. Sutton, fearing the Yaquis might have closed the gap that separated them, back-tracked half a hundred paces, then pulled off trail a short distance; they would see the Indians first now, should they pass.

Choosing a place in a pocket of rocks and brush, they settled down, ate a little of the greasy meat and drank sparingly of the water. They could afford to be generous with their supply only if there was some assurance the Carretas River would be flowing; but there had been doubt in Celestino Bernal's mind, and Sutton refused to accept the risk.

"Get some sleep," he told the deputy after they had

finished the meal. "I'll stand watch."

Gerlay stretched out wearily. "How long you figure we can lay up?"

"An hour. Means thirty minutes each."

"Hardly worth it," Gerlay muttered, and was immediately asleep.

Sutton crossed to the edge of the pocket, fighting the fatigue that pounded at him relentlessly. He found a hump from which he could see the slope below for a considerable distance, and made himself comfortable. The gray, pre-dawn light made all things fairly distinct and he knew if the Yaquis appeared, he would be instantly aware of it—if he could stay awake. Just what he would do if the Indians showed up, he was unsure; the only weapon between Gerlay and himself was the knife he had taken from the Yaqui back in the camp.

The minutes dragged by uneventfully. When he judged the half hour over, he crawled to where Gerlay lay and shook him into wakefulness.

The deputy came up quickly, badly startled. "What's wrong?"

"Your turn," Jack replied, lying down on the hard ground. "Don't let me sleep more'n thirty minutes."

"Hardly closed my eyes," Gerlay said tiredly. "See anything?"

"Nothing—"

The faint, rolling sound of a rifle shot floated hollowly across the canyons. Jack sat up, listened. The report seemed to have originated from somewhere above and to the south of them, but it was difficult to be certain. Ben glanced uneasily at Sutton.

"The Bernals?"

No second shot came. Jack lay back, closed his eyes. "Could be. The Yaquis could've been firing to stop them—they won't kill—can't collect on a dead man."

"Poor devils. Kind of liked them two. Been better if they'd stayed with us."

"We're not out of it yet," Sutton said. "My guess is the Indians split up where the trail divided. Some followed the Bernals, other's will be tracking us."

Jack was asleep the next moment, and seemingly, awake the next. He stared at Gerlay as he sat up, dazed and stupid from exhaustion—and then all came back to him in a rush. Scrambling to his feet, he asked, "Any sign of them?"

"No, nothing," Gerlay replied.

Jack picked up his water bag and slung it over his shoulder. "Let's move out," he said and started to climb the slope of the pocket. "Hear any more gunshots?"

"Only that one."

It could mean little, or it could mean much. Of only one thing could he be certain: the Indians would not kill the Bernals although the two men undoubtedly would be better off if they did stop fatal bullets. Dragged back half alive to the Mariposa, they would spend the rest of their sentences on punishment details.

They pushed on, now staying clear of the more

easily traveled trail, preferring the concealment of the rocks and brush. The day's heat was already making itself felt and as the tall, grotesque shapes of agaves and scarlet-tipped ocotillos became more plentiful, Jack realized they were moving steadily into the Chihuahua Desert.

He glanced to the sky and mopped the sweat clothing his face with the back of his hand. There were no clouds and to hope for one of the infrequent rain showers was ridiculous. He heard Gerlay mutter something, heard also the slosh of water as the deputy took a drink from his bag. He started to caution the man, but decided against it. Gerlay understood what they were up against, and he was no greenhorn to the torture of thirst.

Where were the Yaquis?

Time after time Sutton threw a look over his shoulder to their back trail. There should have been some indication of the Indians' whereabouts. His searching, however, failed to turn up the slightest evidence of their presence. Except for a broad winged eagle soaring in the hot, empty sky, he and Ben Gerlay seemed to be the only living things in the area.

The hours wore on, fierce with a blazing heat that burned all moisture from their bodies and gradually wore down their strength. But they kept on, driven by the recollection of what lay behind them, of what the future held if the Yaquis overtook them and effected their capture.

Many times during the sun scoured hours they

paused to rest, never squandering more than a few minutes, collapsing where they stood—sometimes upon the glittering sand, other times fortunate to find the negligent shade of a smoke tree or some lesser shrub.

The rancid water in the skin bags turned hot, and tasted of decay, making it almost impossible to swallow; they drank it nevertheless. The meat Sutton threw away. He was unable to keep the greasy salty mess on his stomach and after heaving up the bit he ate at midday, he discarded the remainder without regret. Ben Gerlay had no better experience and tossed his portions aside also.

They reached the narrow, sandy wash of the Carretas well before sundown and found it dry. It was no great shock to Jack Sutton, although a disappointment. It hit Gerlay hard. His canteen was almost empty. He sank down on the river's bed, aimlessly scuffing the sand with the toe of his boot.

"Should've known. Never no water in this damned country." He stared off into the layers of heat quivering above the toneless brown and gray of the desert. "We ain't going to make it, Marshal."

Sutton's voice was a dry rasp. "We'll make it. Be cool soon, and I've still got a little water."

"Enough for us both?"

Jack considered the question, thought of how the deputy had squandered his supply. After a moment he said, "Enough."

Gerlay promptly raised his container to his lips and

drained it of its last swallow. Tossing the bag away, he looked at Sutton.

"We staying here 'til dark?"

Jack shrugged, moved to where he could rest himself against the low bank of the river. "Good a place as any."

"How far you think it is to Carneros?"

Sutton scrubbed at the sweat setting up an itch in his beard. "Ought to make it by morning."

"If the Yaquis don't catch up," Gerlay said.

Jack said nothing. He was still puzzled by the failure of the Indians to follow. It was possible, of course, that the party had all turned onto the trail left by Celestino and Eduardo Bernal, and pursued them up the mountain. The Yaquis would not have known how many prisoners were in on the escape; they could have thought it involved only the two brothers.

But that didn't seem reasonable. The Yaqui Indians had no equal when it came to tracking and they would have quickly discovered that more than two men had fled along the trail north from their camp. They would also have noticed when the escaping party had divided. There had to be another explanation.

They found the answer before dawn the next morning.

Traveling hard, they had made good time during the cool hours of the night, following the sandy track of the empty Carretas. When the first hint of day brightened the eastern sky, they caught sight of the village etched darkly on the crown of a small hill. Tired, hungry, and worn, they halted on a half buried thrust of rock for a final rest period—and then the dry cough of a man brought both to their feet.

"Ahead of us," Sutton warned, sinking to his knees and pulling the deputy with him. "In that stand of mesquite."

Thankful for the half dark, they doubled back and circled, abandoning the river bed for a shallow arroyo that sliced off at an angle. Drawing abreast the scatter of yellow-flowered shrubs, they dropped to their bellies and wormed their way in closer.

Six Yaquis were hunched in the brush. Sutton understood instantly why there had been no trackers nipping at their heels: the Indians had realized they were making for Carneros—there was no other logical choice. Tireless runners, they had simply cut directly across the desert, ignoring the round-about route that skirted the mountain, and reached the settlement well ahead of their objectives and set up an ambush.

"Just waiting." Ben Gerlay groaned. "If that gut-eater hadn't coughed, we'd of walked right into their trap."

Sutton was silent as he studied the Indians. After a moment he began to work his way back to the arroyo. They had been careless—he should have remembered, and heeded, Celestino Bernal's warning. Luckily no damage was done.

"What do we do?" Gerlay asked when they were again well hidden in the sandy wash. "Nothing but open ground between us and the town. They'll spot us the minute we make a move."

Jack Sutton raised his eyes to the sky, now streaked with yellow and orange fingers of light. That he and the deputy could not withstand another day on the desert was apparent; neither had tasted decent food in days—and their water was almost gone. Weariness clung to them like lead weights. It would be easy to not resist, to just lie down, suffer out the terrible heat—and let nature and the elements bring an end to all problems. But Jack Sutton refused to accept that solution. His life and that of the deputy were not the only ones involved; there was still Billy, waiting help-lessly, while the shadow of the gallows falling across his cell window grew taller with each passing day.

"We chance it," he said.

X

BEN GERLAY SWORE QUIETLY. "NOTHING ELSE WE CAN do?"

"Nothing—unless you want to lay here and roast," Jack replied. "Those Yaquis will wait all day—longer if they have to."

The deputy shook his head doubtfully, still staring off toward the village. "Even if we get by the Indians, we got that *commandante*—Torrero—to worry about."

"Same odds—and I figure it's worth the chance."

Sutton paused, adding, "You've got the right to do what you want—I have to make a try. Billy's time's running short and it's up to me to find Stinger Jones. It won't matter if you don't come along; I know what he looks like."

Ben Gerlay swung his gray eyes to Sutton, and studied the lawman briefly. He shrugged. "Reckon it's the only thing we can do. What've you got in mind?"

"It's maybe a mile to the town. We'll follow this wash—"

"Hell—takes us in the wrong direction!"

"I know that, but it also leads us away from the Indians. When we reach the end of it, maybe there'll be another that'll angle the opposite way."

The deputy sighed. "Seems like we're always depending on something doing something. . . ."

Sutton smiled faintly, and through talking, moved off up the arroyo. Gerlay immediately got to his feet and dropped in behind.

Crouched and walking fast to take advantage of the semi-darkness, Jack pursued the course of the sandy bed as it slanted to the northwest, leading them away, as the deputy had pointed out, from the village. But a few hundred yards later it began to curve back.

Hope lifted within Sutton, but it was short lived; abruptly the arroyo petered out. Halting where there was still some depth, Jack crossed to the edge and looked back. The mesquite where the Yaquis waited was clearly visible.

"Don't seem to be much better off," Gerlay said,

squatting on his heels. "We try something else?"

Sutton turned his attention to the country ahead. From the arroyo's termination there was only a slight roll of land, and then the flat fell away behind a fairly high dune. Calculating the length and contour of the formation, Jack guessed it would afford them cover for considerable distance—sufficient to permit their reaching Carneros unseen by the Yaquis—if they could get to it. There lay the problem.

He considered it for a short time and then, saying nothing to the deputy, he stepped back to the center of the wash and looked around for brush. Along the far side in a deep gouge, he saw several clumps of Apache plume. Drawing his knife, he cut two branches of good size, tossed one to Gerlay.

The deputy frowned. "What's this for?"

"We've got about two hundred yards of open ground to cross," Jack explained. "Put that bush on your back and crawl. Maybe we'll fool the Indians."

Thrusting the base of the shrub under his belt to hold it in place, Sutton dropped to the ground and began to pull himself out of the arroyo.

"Take it slow," he said over his shoulder.

Gerlay grunted a reply and they moved off. The flat had a higher roll than Jack had thought—actually a slight hump—and before they had covered a quarter of the distance, he realized they were on full display for the Yaquis if any happened to pay more than casual notice.

The sun broke above the horizon and the heat at

110

once set in. He heard the deputy mutter a curse as he raked his hand against a slab of prickly pear. Sutton grinned in spite of himself at the flow of vivid words.

A thought came to him. A great deal of time had been lost—and Henry Parmalee could be getting anxious. Since he no longer needed Gerlay to identify Stinger Jones, it would be wise to send him on to Trailbreak, and have him explain to the jurist what had happened. Such personal intercession on the part of the deputy would guarantee more time for Billy. He'd do that, Jack decided—if and when they reached Carneros and again had horses.

Laboring for breath, Sutton halted and glanced to the south. The clumps of mesquite were yet in sight. One of the Indians had risen and was wandering aimlessly about.

"Don't mover" He barked the warning at Gerlay.

The deputy froze. Jack watched the slim, dark shape of the Yaqui through shuttered eyes. Finally the man sat down.

"Let's go," Sutton said immediately, and resumed the tedious crawling.

"For Christ's sake—how much farther?" Gerlay asked in an exhausted voice.

"Fifty yards."

The distance was less. Sutton became aware of the hump's dropping away and increased his efforts. He looked back. The mesquite thicket was no longer visible. He crawled a dozen more lengths for good measure, rolled over and sat up. Discarding the wiry shrub with its feathery balls, he looked at Gerlay. The deputy grinned wolfishly.

"By God—we made it."

Sutton nodded, took a deep breath, and got to his feet. His strained muscles protested the action but he ignored the pain, and glanced toward the settlement. They were north of it now, and the dune curved gracefully in to meet the scatter of sunbaked huts on their blind side. They would have no difficulty approaching.

Jack tossed away his water bag, spurning the few remaining swallows of brackish water; he could satisfy his thirst when they reached the settlement.

"Come on," he said, and struck off at a fast walk.

An hour later they lay in the shade of a crumbling adobe wall and studied the headquarters of Juan Torrero. They had experienced no problems entering the village as it was still early and few residents were up and about.

No activities were apparent in the *rurale* base. Jack could see his bay horse in the small corral at the rear of the buildings. Gerlay's black was not with him, being, possibly, inside the small barn standing at the back of the yard. If any of the *commandante's* men were awake, they were keeping to their quarters.

"Be a chore getting in there," Gerlay observed. "Might be smart to just grab us a couple of horses from somebody else's corral."

"We need guns—and the money Torrero took from

us," Jack answered. "Doubt if anybody else around here has horses, anyway."

"How we going to work it?"

Jack shrugged. When in doubt, use the direct approach. "We get up and walk right in."

The deputy stared at him with open mouth. "Just go busting right in there?"

"Office is likely deserted this early."

"Looks like the whole place is."

"The moment we're inside, get your hands on a couple of guns—they'll be hanging on that rack behind Torrero's desk. If it happens somebody's in there, leave them to me. You get the guns. Understand?"

Gerlay nodded. "I'll get them."

Sutton rose to his feet. It was a long gamble but he could see no other means for fulfilling their needs—and it should be done before the *rurales* were all up and wandering about. He glanced along the huts. A woman was hanging clothes on a line stretched between two trees on the far side of the street. No one else was in sight.

"Let's go," he said and walked boldly into the open, heading for the door to Torrero's office.

Reaching it he halted and listened briefly. He could hear nothing. Drawing his knife, Jack threw a look at Gerlay and opened the door. A low sigh slipped from his lips as he stepped inside. The room was empty.

"Guns," he reminded Gerlay in a soft whisper, and moved in behind the *commandante's* desk.

He found his own belt hanging on a peg, pistol still in the holster, and strapped it on. As he was checking the weapon for loads, he heard Gerlay speak.

"Where you reckon he keeps the money?"

"Probably carries it on—" Jack began, and hushed abruptly.

One of the two inner doors opened. A soldier entered, face tipped down. Jack crossed over fast, pistol in hand. As the startled Mexican looked up, Sutton jammed the barrel into his belly.

"No noise!"

The *rurale* nodded, his eyes spreading into large circles.

"Torrero—where is he?"

The soldier drew back. "No—I fear—"

"It is wiser to fear me!" Sutton snarled. "Speak, or you are dead!"

"The *commandante*—in his quarters—"

"Guide us there."

Again the solider recoiled. "No—I dare not!"

Sutton jabbed the man cruelly with his pistol. "You will do so, or I shoot!"

The soldier nodded woodenly. He turned, halted as Gerlay stepped up to relieve him of his pistol. Sutton dug hard with his weapon. The *rurale* groaned, crossed hurriedly to the adjacent inner door and opened it.

Sutton crowded him close, never once letting up on the pressure he exerted. Gerlay, now with a gun in either hand, followed, keeping an eye to their rear. They entered a small patio and halted before a deep-set entrance in the opposite wall. The soldier, his face distorted, cringed, turned to Jack.

"I cannot! The *commandante*—he is indisposed—"

"Indisposed—hell!" Sutton rasped and booted the door open.

A woman's startled scream greeted him. Shoving the *rurale* ahead, he plunged into the room. Torrero shouted an oath and the girl grabbed at a bed cover with which to clothe her nakedness, leaped up and darted into a far corner.

"What is the meaning—" the officer began, his black eyes furious, and then the question died as he recognized Sutton and Ben Gerlay. "You!" he gasped in a strangled voice. "How—"

"It is not important," Jack snapped. He pointed at the cowering girl. "Stand with her. You, also," he added, giving the soldier a push. "Tie them up, Ben. Use a gag."

Torrero, struggling with his tight breeches, crossed to the corner. Anger still brightened his eyes and his mouth was a hard, thin line.

"What is it you want?" he demanded.

"Our horses," Sutton answered. "Also the money taken from us."

"Ought to collect a little extry," the deputy said, ripping a blanket into strips. "I ain't forgetting what he done to us."

He moved to where the three stood, and began first to bind the wrists of the officer. There was no gentleness in his method; time and again he slammed the *commandante* against the unyielding wall of the room.

"Where is the money?" Jack asked.

Torrero shook his head. "It is gone—"

"Better not be!" Gerlay snarled, and struck him a backhand blow across the mouth. "Talk!"

The officer staggered and spat blood. "The drawer—" he said, pointing with his chin at a chest standing against a far wall. "There is gold in a small pouch. Take what is yours."

Sutton wheeled to the chest. They were pushing their luck, he knew; all of Torrero's men would soon be up and moving about. He reached for the drawer, and yanked it open. Locating the pouch, he dumped its contents of gold pieces onto the bed. Counting out the amount the officer had taken from him, he thrust the coins into his pocket and stepped to where the deputy was at that moment binding the soldier.

"Get your money," he said. "I'll finish."

He completed the task and ordered all three to lie on the floor. After he had bound their ankles, Jack reached up and pulled Torrero's gag free.

"All the time at the Mariposa I thought of the day when I could return and slit your throat," he said, drawing his knife and touching the tip to the officer's neck. "It would give me great pleasure—and do your country and mine a favor. But I have decided against it, on one condition."

Torrero stared at him. "What is this condition?"

"The man—Stinger Jones—where is he?"

The *commandante* shook his head. "This I do not know."

"He is not in the village?"

"No."

Sutton twisted the knife slightly. Torrero muttered an oath, and jerked away, a spot of blood on his throat.

"It is the truth!" he cried. "Even the knife cannot force me to tell—for I do not know! He rode from here after speaking of Nogales. Perhaps he went there."

Nogales—one hundred and fifty long miles up the border. Jack sighed heavily, replacing Torrero's gag. Rising, he looked down at the officer. "If you lie—"

The *commandante* shook his head frantically and cast a hurried glance at the soldier who nodded a vigorous confirmation. Sutton turned and looked questioningly at Ben Gerlay.

"All set," the deputy said. "Corral's at the end of the yard—saw it when we came in."

Jack crossed to Gerlay's side, and paused to face Torrero and the others. "Do not move for a half hour and make no sounds. We will be near."

Following Gerlay into the patio, he pulled the door shut. The deputy touched his arm.

"Somebody in the office. I heard them rustling around—" Jack nodded. They must move fast—and with care. The entire garrison could be abroad by that hour. He crossed quickly to the low gate at the end of the courtyard. It opened into a narrow, alley-like passageway that led into Torrero's private corral.

They covered that distance without interruption and entered the walled-in yard. Sutton's bay lifted an inquiring head, then whickered softly. Jack hurried to him, and led him to the shed where tack was kept. Ben Gerlay was there before him searching for his own mount. He met Jack at the half door.

"Black of mine ain't here. Gear's gone, too."

Sutton, locating his equipment, moved impatiently. "Pick yourself another—and hurry. We don't have much time."

Gerlay selected a tall sorrel, found the necessary gear, and got the horse ready for traveling. While he waited, Jack checked his rifle, saw that it was still fully loaded, and then turned to filling the canteens from the water trough. He was trying to recall the layout of the town and the relation of Torrero's headquarters to the road leading out. If they turned left once they were outside the yard, they should be headed in the proper direction, he thought.

The deputy came up, leading the big sorrel. Sutton handed him a canteen. "Soon as we're clear of town, I'll line out for Nogales. You go back to Trailbreak—explain to Parmalee what held us up—"

"Yaquis!" Gerlay blurted, eyes reaching past Sutton to the street. "Bastards are onto us!"

Jack whirled. Over the top of the corral wall he could see two Indians moving along the dusty street, dark heads swinging from side to side as they searched. There would be others scattered throughout the village.

He spun to the gate, slid the bar and led the bay into the runway. Gerlay followed closely. Once outside, Jack stepped to the saddle.

"Circle town," he said in a tense voice. "Got to dodge them."

The deputy nodded tautly. Sutton guided his horse down the narrow passage, then cut left. A few huts lay before him and, gun in hand, he walked the bay around them quietly.

Reaching the last, he veered off. They would have to cross the street where they had seen the Yaquis—and this he would like to accomplish unnoticed, if possible. It was not that he feared the Indians—both he and Ben Gerlay were well armed—but an encounter would instantly arouse Torrero's *rurales* and more delay would ensue.

They reached the street. Jack halted, holding the bay close to a clump of brush that shielded him from view. He threw his glance along the dusty strip. An Indian was leaning against a wall about midway; no others were in sight.

Beckoning to the deputy, he touched the bay with his heels and started across. As he reached the opposite side, a dry, scuffing sound caught his attention and sent alarm racing through him. He whirled. Behind Ben Gerlay an Indian had appeared in the narrow area separating two of the huts.

The Yaqui's leathery face was set and a bright red scarf—Eduardo Bernal's scarf—encircled his head, holding his coarse, black hair in place. A rifle was at his shoulder as he drew bead on the deputy.

"Look out!" Sutton yelled, and drew fast.

He tumbled a quick shot as Gerlay threw himself to one side. The Yaqui, jolted from the impact of Jack's bullet, staggered back, discharging the rifle.

Yells went up from the direction of Torrero's headquarters and immediately two soldiers ran into the open. Farther down the street the lone Indian had been joined by two more and all were staring.

"You hit?" Jack yelled at the deputy as he urged the bay on.

Gerlay, his face chalky, grinned and lashed the sorrel to Sutton's side. "It was close. . . . Which way?"

"Straight ahead!" the lawman answered, and crouched low.

XI

THEY RODE HARD, TAKING THE SAME ROUTE ALONG THE dune they had followed earlier on foot. When they broke clear of its rippled length, Jack Sutton glanced over his shoulder. Five soldiers, strung out in a ragged line, were streaming along the foot of the sandy roll. Some distance behind them a sixth rider was flogging his mount to catch up. . . . That would be Torrero, finally free and clothed, now rushing to assume command of the chase.

Jack yelled at Gerlay, and pointed to the *rurales.*

The deputy turned his head, studied the oncoming riders and swung back to face Sutton.

"Going to have us a race!" he yelled, grinning.

Sutton hunched forward on the bay and called upon him for more speed. It was tough going for the horse in the loose sand, but the several days in Torrero's corral had afforded him rest and good feed. He was in excellent condition.

The ground began to lift as they drew near a small range of mountains—the Espuelos, he recalled, and remembered, too, that they lay close to the border. If he and the deputy could hold their lead on the soldiers until they were on the opposite side of the rocky hills, the pursuit would end: Torrero would not risk breaching the border just to salve his wounded dignity.

Jack looked back again when they reached the base of the Espuelos and started up a narrow, hard packed trail. The *commandante* had overtaken his men, and now rode out in front; they had not been able to shorten the gap to any appreciable extent. Sutton settled in satisfaction on the now sweating bay; with no bad luck Torrero and his *rurales* would soon give it up. He could forget them.

Late in the morning of the third day following the escape from Carneros, Sutton and Ben Gerlay rode into Nogales—bearded, fierce looking men, gaunt from hunger and weariness. They had shaken Torrero, as Jack had anticipated, when they swung across the border, and had seen no more of him or his men during the exhausting ride to the brawling settlement that straddled the line dividing the two countries.

They halted at the first livery stable they encountered and immediately made use of the water trough, first dousing their heads, then stripping to the waist and washing themselves of the dust and sweat that caked their bodies.

"Going to get me a whole bath soon as I can," Gerlay said, scrubbing at his stubbled chin. "And a barber shop shave."

Sutton was only half listening. He could use both himself, and the odor from his body was so bad he could hardly stand it—but he had more important business on his mind: Stinger Jones. He should now get a letter off to Henry Parmalee, since his plan to send Gerlay back had blown up when Torrero and his soldiers took a hand in their flight.

The time limit for Billy would be drawing dangerously close, but word to Parmalee would delay things for a few more days. Nogales was on the regular mail run and a letter posted there would likely arrive in Trailbreak in less time than it would take the deputy to make the ride, anyway. He'd get the message written immediately, he decided, pulling on his shirt.

A graying man leaning against the door frame of the stable removed a blackened pipe from his lips, cocked his head to one side, spat, and glared at them.

"Now that you've just plain helped yourself to my water—how about them horses? Want them looked after?"

Jack smiled, said, "Be obliged to you. Where's the stage stop?"

The liveryman slouched forward, gathered up the reins of the two horses. "Other end of town—ain't far. Keep going down the street."

Gerlay glanced at Sutton. "What are you wanting the stage stop for?"

"Sending a letter to the judge, to ask him for more time."

The deputy thought for a moment. "Good idea," he said, and put his attention on the hostler. "There a place to eat around here close?"

"Sure, about half way down. Best dang grub in town. Wife runs it."

The deputy nodded, again faced Jack. "What say we go there first? I'm hungry as hell. You can do your letter writing while we wait."

It was good thinking. The quicker they got their necessary side chores out of the way, the sooner they could start digging out Stinger Jones.

They located the restaurant—the front part of a residence altered to accommodate half a dozen tables with chairs, and ordered a full meal of steak, potatoes and all the trimmings. Neither man had enjoyed good food in days.

Jack obtained paper, pencil and envelope from the woman who waited on them—the stable owner's wife, he assumed—and while their orders were being prepared, began the note to Henry Parmalee. In it he set forth in detail the cause of their delay and advised the jurist they were, hopefully, on the verge of arresting Jones. He continued to work on the letter even after the food was placed before them, and by the time he had finished, Ben Gerlay had already downed his meal and was sitting idly by.

The deputy watched him seal the envelope, then reached for it. "Can save some time. I'll trot this over to the stage depot while you eat."

Jack surrendered the letter. "Be fine. I was just thinking—we ought to check with that hostler, too. Stinger might've stopped there first when he rode in."

Ben Gerlay rose. "I'll do it," he said and turned to the door.

Jack resumed his meal, savoring the excellent food, grateful for the moments of absolute relaxation away from the harsh pressures that beset him. For the moment, he had done all he could for Billy—and his efforts should prove sufficient. Henry Parmalee wouldn't refuse to grant extra time, considering the cause for the delay. And the search could be drawing to a close, he thought, sipping at his third cup of black coffee. Stinger Jones was most likely still in Nogales; it was the sort of town he'd like.

He glanced up. Through the spotlessly clean glass of the window he saw Gerlay walking up the street. He was on his way back from the stage depot and en route now to the livery stable. Ben was a pretty good man to have along; the two of them working together had covered a lot of ground—and it was always a big advantage to have someone watching your back when things got tight.

He drained the last of his coffee, sighed, and got to his feet. Paying the check, he moved out into the blistering heat. Looking toward the livery barn, he saw Gerlay round the corner of the sprawling structure and head his way.

"Stinger's here," the deputy said, brushing at the sweat on his face. "Hostler said he come by several days ago. Asked about a place to sleep. The old man sent him down to the Bellrope—hotel somewhere close to the line."

Sutton, pulse quickening, stared off down the street. "He seen anything of him since?"

"Says he ain't laid eyes on him but figures he's still around. Never saw him ride out."

"Let's find this Bellrope place," Sutton said and abruptly wheeled about.

It proved to be a combination hotel and saloon. Jack went directly to the aging clerk at the desk, and stated his needs.

"I know him," the man replied.

Sutton waited for him to continue. When no more was said, he slapped the desk impatiently. "Where is he? It's important I see him."

"Important I see him, too," the old man answered with infuriating disinterest. "Hotel bill's owing. If you're a friend of his'n, maybe you'd like to pay his bill."

"Looking for him, not his bills," Jack said. "When did you last see him?"

"Three nights ago, in the saloon. Was going across

the line, so he said. Had found hisself a woman over there he was right keen about."

"He didn't come back?"

The clerk wagged his head. "Not far as I know."

"Must still be over there. What's this woman's name?"

The old man shrugged. "Don't have no traffic with them hookers, so I wouldn't know. Ask Gus—the bartender—he's a sort of friend of Jones."

Sutton and Gerlay cut back across the lobby to the broad, square room that served as a saloon. It was cool and shadowy, with only half a dozen patrons at that hour of the day. They halted at the long counter and Jack repeated his question to the balding man wiping glasses.

"Sure, name's Crucita," he said. "Real looker. Stinger was all fired up over her." Leaning forward, Gus pointed to the clerk. "The old man bitchin' about Stinger's bill?"

Gerlay laughed. "Wanted us to pay it."

The bartender swore. "He'll try anything to collect his stinking bills. Hell, Stinger'll pay. He'll get fed up with that woman and come back."

"You figure he's still over there then."

Gus nodded. "I'd a seen him if he'd come back. And something else—he wouldn't dodge no two-bit hotel bill. Old Stinger's got plenty of money."

"So we heard," Gerlay said drily.

"How do we find this Crucita?" Sutton asked. "You know?"

"Who don't?" the bartender grunted. "Just cross the

line, turn right at the first corner—they call it Crib Alley. Her's is the fourth shack."

Sutton and the deputy returned to the street. Pausing briefly to get his bearings, Jack angled toward the scatter of low roofed structures a few hundred yards to their right. A small mound of stones and a sagging wire fence marked the actual location of the border.

Sutton, recalling Gerlay's earlier reluctance to enter Mexico, glanced at the deputy. "Be a good time to get that bath and shave if you're of a mind. I can handle Stinger."

Ben shrugged. "Ain't anxious to cross that line again, but I reckon I'll stick with you, Marshal."

Jack nodded, and continued on with the deputy at his shoulder. They walked by the marker and the small sentry hut just beyond it where a guard in a sweat stained uniform stared sleepily at them, and came to the corner of Crib Alley. Turning right, they made their way to the fourth hut, a small, board affair with blinds drawn tight over the windows.

Jack and Gerlay halted at the door. The deputy drew his pistol and pulled the hammer to full cock position. Sutton laid a hand on the man's arm.

"Remember—I want him alive," he said in a low voice.

"Just aim to be careful."

Jack reached for the knob and twisted it slightly. The door was locked. Gerlay moved up, raised his leg and drove a booted foot against the panel. It flew inward with a splintering crash.

Propelled by momentum, the deputy plunged into the shadowy interior of the room. Sutton was at his heels and together they came to a halt. The place was small, and barren except for a table, two chairs and a row of shelving on one wall that supported a meager selection of groceries. The air was stifling, reeking of spilled whiskey and perfume.

A groan came from an adjoining area. Sutton and Gerlay moved cautiously to the connecting doorway from which a coarse portiere hung. The deputy drew the limp cloth aside and they peered into the dimness. A woman lay across the bed. She was alone.

Jack crossed over, threw up the shade and opened a window, admitting a gust of fresh air. Crucita moaned again, and struggled to sit up. She wore only a loose, soiled wrapper and under it her skin was a mass of dark, angry bruises. Her face, probably once pretty, was swollen out of shape and her hair hung about slumped shoulders in a tangled mat.

"Drink . . ." she mumbled. "In the name of the Holy Mother—"

Exhausted, she sank back into the rumpled, foul smelling bed clothes. Gerlay hunted about, found a bottle in which remained one or two swallows of whiskey. She gulped it down greedily without raising her head.

"Who did this to you?" Sutton asked in Spanish. "It was Stinger Jones who beat you?"

Crucita's puffed eye lids parted slightly. She stared uncertainly at Jack. "Who—who is it that speaks?"

128

"I am called Sutton. Was it Stinger who beat you?"

She bobbed her head weakly. "Stinger. He is one sonofabitch. He beats me, and no pay nothing. . . . One sonofabitch."

"Seems old Stinger don't believe in paying for anything," Gerlay said with a laugh.

Jack reached again for the woman's shoulder, shook her until her eyes opened again. "Stinger—where is he now?"

"Where?" she echoed stupidly. "Where? Tucson, maybe. He talks of a woman there. . . . This I not like. I tell him go . . . haul his ass from here, go to his Tucson woman. He get mad—beat me—Christ! He was a crazy one! He not stop. I think he kill me. . . ." She paused, raised her head. "The bottle—is there no more?"

Gerlay said, "It's dry."

Sutton reached into his pocket for coins. "Get her a quart," he said, handing them to the deputy. "Saw a saloon just around the corner."

Gerlay turned back into the adjoining room. Jack shook Crucita once more. "My friend goes for a bottle. He will return soon."

She focused her bleary eyes on him. "You are a friend of Stinger's, no?"

"I only seek him. When did this happen? When did he beat you?"

She stared at Sutton with the unseeing, unwavering gaze of a hopeless alcoholic. "I do not know this. One night, two nights ago. Someone knock on the door last

129

night—I could not answer. It was the night ahead—yes—the night ahead. . . ."

She closed her lids, and settled deeper into the bed. Sutton got to his feet and walked to the window. Tucson. A good day's ride—another one lost. And maybe Stinger had kept on riding. He could almost feel the noose tightening around Billy's neck; it was almost as if it were about his own.

Gerlay's boots crunched in the yard. Sutton turned and watched the deputy enter and lean over the woman.

"Here, you old sot," he said, forcing the bottle into her fingers. "This'll make you forget all your aches and pains."

Crucita clutched the whiskey, pressing it to her bruised lips. She took a long, gulping swallow and sighed contentedly. *"Gracias, gracias—"*

"Find out anything else?"

At Gerlay's question Sutton looked up. "Thinks it was night before last when Stinger pulled out."

"For Tucson. You believe her?"

"Must have said something that made her think that . . . stuck in her mind. Anyway—it's all we've got."

Jack crossed through the rooms and moved out into the yard with Gerlay at his heels. They stopped, both men grateful for the clean, if hot, air.

"Let's stay here tonight," the deputy suggested as they strode toward the street. "Bed sure would feel good—same's a bath and shave."

Sutton was shaking his head even before Gerlay had finished speaking. "We're only a couple of days behind Stinger. Smart to keep after him."

They reached the corner and turned for the border. An officer and two *rurales* on dust caked horses had pulled up before the guard's hut, and were speaking to the now thoroughly awake man.

"Torrero!" Sutton blurted in surprise, and jerked back into the thorny protection of a wild rose bush.

It was hard to believe—and understand. The Mexican *commandante* had followed them all the way to Nogales, apparently keeping to his side of the border. Juan Torrero was a bold and foolish man. He surely realized he would be putting his own neck on the block if he pushed charges.

"We better pull out fast," Ben Gerlay said in a strained voice. "He grabs us here, we're done for."

The deputy was right. If Torrero caught them in Mexico he wouldn't worry about facing charges— he'd have everything his own way. Sutton edged forward, peered around the prickly clump. The *commandante* and his two men were coming toward them, walking their horses slowly, quietly. Evidently the guard had told the officer the direction taken by the two men described to him.

Jack withdrew and motioned to Gerlay for silence. Bending low, he led the way back to the first of the huts, passing along its side to the rear. Halting, he again glanced to the street. He could see only the top of the sentry box.

Sutton touched the deputy's arm and pointed to the small, slant-roofed cubicle. "Give Torrero time to reach the corner, then we make for that."

Gerlay nodded. "Mex sure don't give up easy."

"Can't figure him," Jack said. "All we did was take back what was ours—and spoil his little party."

The deputy chuckled. "Maybe I run off with his best horse."

"He got your black. Pretty even trade." Jack looked to the street. "Can't see them. Ought to be at the corner by now."

They moved off at once, slicing diagonally across the littered yard behind the shacks and entering the street a few paces short of the sentry hut. As they stepped into the open, Sutton glanced over his shoulder. Torrero and his men had stopped at the intersection and were looking down Crib Alley.

"Commandante!"

The sudden yell of the guard brought Sutton around. Gerlay spat an oath and threw himself at the man who was endeavoring to get his pistol clear of its holster.

"Commandante! Aquí! Aquí!"

Sutton spun as Torrero and his men wheeled and started up the street at a fast gallop. He rushed to Gerlay's side and drove his fist into the guard's jaw. It broke the man's death-like grip on the deputy's arm.

"Run!" he shouted, and legged it for the marker.

XII

THEY CROSSED THE LINE AND SWUNG LEFT FOR A saloon standing a few paces distant. Jack could hear the guard still shouting, and in the background, the quick hammer of Torrero's horses as he and his men answered the man's frantic summons.

They reached the saloon and wheeled toward the door. A man wearing an army uniform came through hurriedly, almost colliding with Sutton. Apparently he was the American representative at the border's entrance, and had been inside taking time for a drink when Jack and Ben Gerlay had passed through.

"What's all the yelling?" he asked, not slowing his stride.

"Mexican guard got knocked flat," Sutton replied, pushing on into the building.

With the deputy at his side, he crossed the small room, aiming for a door in the opposite wall. Opening it, they stepped out into the sunlight again, to find themselves in a passageway that lay between the saloon and its adjacent neighbor. Jack doubled along its length, and halted at the corner facing the street. He looked toward the border.

Torrero had dismounted and was in conversation with the American guard. Jack wondered what was being said, speculated on the possibility of the *rurale* officer making some sort of charge. Torrero could come up with one legitimate complaint—the attack on the Mexican guard. Most likely that would be as far as he dare go. He could, of course, ask permission to enter and make a search for the two Americans, using the guard incident as a mask for his real intentions, whatever they were.

It was doubtful if approval would be forthcoming. The treaty between the two countries was explicit on such matters and it was beyond the power of any ordinary guard to grant it. A request would require written confirmation from official sources—a procedure that involved a vast amount of red tape. But refusal by the guard would not stop Torrero if he were determined to enter the United States; he had only to go a short distance below or above the settlement and cross the line unnoticed.

Gerlay pointed to the group. The American guard had turned, and was staring toward the saloon. "Let's get the hell out of here—he's got us pegged."

Jack nodded. Evidently the guard, after listening to a description of the two men who had perpetrated the attack on his Mexican counterpart, was remembering the pair with whom he had almost collided, and was adding two and two and coming up with an answer.

Jack turned to head back along the passageway. "Better circle around, get to that livery stable from the back."

"Then what?"

"Head for Tucson."

The deputy sighed. "Going to be a hot ride."

"Be hotter if that guard turns us over to Torrero," Sutton said drily, and hurried on.

They were in the saddle half an hour later, taking a road that angled east for the Patagonia Mountains. They reached the western tip of that range around the middle of the afternoon, and then began veering off for the towering mass of Baldy Peak, at the end of the Santa Ritas.

They would rest there a few hours—until midnight, Jack decided, and then push on for Tucson. That would bring them to the settlement around sunrise. Neither of them had taken much rest since the uncomfortable nights in the hut at the Mariposa, and when he faced Stinger Jones he wanted to be at his best.

They rode in silence through the blasting desert heat, each occupied by his own thoughts. Jack tried to calculate the time that had elapsed since they rode from Trailbreak, but found it all a jumbled haze; that he still had a few days seemed probable. And those, plus the additional time he had requested of Parmalee, should make it possible to capture Stinger and return within the deadline.

But if Stinger Jones was not in Tucson?

He considered that at length, and realized he would have no course open except to continue the search. It would, however, be necessary to notify Parmalee again, but this time he would dispatch no letter—he would do as he had planned at Carneros, send Ben Gerlay. The deputy, arriving in person with the complete story and fairly good evidence that Stinger had the bank's money, would present something the jurist could scarcely ignore.

"You think Torrero'll be trailing us?"

Gerlay's question brought Sutton from his deep thoughts. He shrugged. "Can't see why."

"Dogged us all the way to Nogales."

"I know that. . . . Still can't understand it."

"Can't see why he's hanging on," the deputy said irritably. "Got paid for us once."

"Something else on his mind," Jack said and fell silent.

As soon as Billy's problems were ironed out he, personally, in order to avoid Federal involvement, intended to report the Mariposa to the Mexican government. It should be made aware of the injustice and barbarism being practiced in its name. He would suggest an investigation be made of not only Kollar's mine but of all other similar institutions; they need only ask in the villages to learn which ones. That was the trouble with Mexican officialdom—it never got around to talking with the common man.

"Could be Torrero's pride that's got him chasing us. *Rurales* set great store by that."

"Maybe. Hardly seems worth jumping the border for though."

"Think we've seen the last of him?"

"Be my guess."

Near sundown they halted in a dry wash on the western slope of the Santa Ritas where deep sand provided a smooth, if hard bed. They were compelled to go supperless as Torrero's men had stripped Sutton's saddlebags of all trail supplies, and the big Mexican saddle appropriated by Gerlay carried no pouches at all. It was no hardship on either man; the fine dinner they had enjoyed at Nogales would satisfy them until they arrived in Tucson.

"No fire," Sutton said, making himself comfortable on the sand, his shoulders against a rock. "Be warm until midnight—then we'll be moving on."

Gerlay abandoned the pile of dry twigs and brush he had been gathering. "Always like having a fire," he murmured. Abruptly he glanced to Jack. "Thought you figured Torrero had given up?"

Sutton smiled faintly at the deputy. "What's eating you? That *commandante* sure got under your hide."

Gerlay wagged his head. "Don't hanker being dragged back to that mine."

"Me either. I was thinking about Apaches."

The deputy stared off into the night. "Heard they was peaceful around here."

"They are, only now and then a party of young bucks out to blood themselves cracks down on some pilgrim. It's not worth taking any chances."

Ben Gerlay seemed relieved. He crossed to where the sorrel stood, and helped himself to a drink of water. The desert before them lay warm and hushed; back up on the ridges of the Santa Ritas an owl hooted forlornly.

Sutton drew his pistol and stretched out full length beside the rock bench. His eyes were heavy and weariness dragged at him. The owl hooted again and he was vaguely aware of Ben Gerlay coming in close and settling down.

Suddenly, he was fully awake. The world about him was bathed in brilliant, silver moonlight and he guessed he must have slept for several hours. He lay absolutely still, speculating on what it was that had awakened him. There appeared to be no one—nothing—visible in the eerie glow, and a complete, dead silence lay over the hills and flats.

Holding himself motionless, he moved only his eyes. Gerlay continued to snore softly, undisturbed by whatever had roused Sutton if, indeed, there was something. And then Jack knew there had been cause: metal clicked against stone. The small sound came from their left, seemingly close to the slope. In the stillness, the noise was abnormally distinct.

Raising his right hand slightly, he picked up a small bit of sand, flipped it at Gerlay. The deputy stirred.

"Ben—"

"Yeah?" Gerlay's answer was a hoarse grunt.

"Somebody coming."

There was a long minute of silence. The deputy said: "Don't hear nothing. Which way?"

"Below us."

Again there was quiet. Far to the north a coyote gave voice; Gerlay's sorrel stamped, blew noisily. Jack's nerves tightened. There was stealthy motion at the mouth of the arroyo. Bracing himself, Sutton lunged to his feet, pistol in hand. Gerlay had seen it too; his actions matched those of Sutton.

Standing side by side, they waited. A rider moved slowly into full view. Moonlight glittered on the braid decorating his uniform.

"Torrero!" Gerlay exclaimed, and brought his weapon to bear fast.

"Have care!" the Mexican shouted. "It will be wise to look behind!"

Jack did not lower his revolver. He ducked his head at the deputy. "Take a look. . . . I'll keep him covered."

He heard Gerlay swear quietly. "It's them two soldiers of his. They've got a bead on us."

"And I've got one on Torrero," Sutton replied, loud enough for all to hear. "They shoot us—I shoot him."

Ben Gerlay laughed, a strained, unnatural sound. "You savvy, *Commandante?* We got us a standoff. Tell your *soldado* to stand easy or you're a dead man!"

Torrero was silent. Finally he shrugged, the movement stirring a pale sparkle in the silvered night. "It would appear there is no advantage for either." He shifted his attention to the slope. "Lower your rifles."

"Ease over to the right—keep your eyes on them," Jack said quietly to Gerlay.

As the deputy drifted almost imperceptibly to the far side of the wash, Sutton took a few steps toward Torrero. "You take much risk, *commandante,* violating the border."

The *rurale* captain laughed. "You joke with me, my friend. Such is done each day—by your countrymen as well as mine."

"True, but it is usual for those of official standing to observe the agreement. If you are on a personal matter it would have been better to remove your uniform and come as a citizen. Is this a matter of personal business? The Mariposa mine, perhaps?"

"I care nothing for the Mariposa," Torrero said stiffly.

"Then what is it that will force an officer of the Mexican army to violate his oath?"

Juan Torrero squirmed uncomfortably under the scathing derisiveness of Sutton's tone.

"If it does not concern the bounty one might collect from mine owners, could it be a matter involving a sorrel horse?"

"He was my finest animal—"

"The black you took from my friend was a good horse, also. I consider it a fair exchange."

"I shall not quarrel over the horse—"

"Then what is it?" Sutton exploded, suddenly tired of the polite fencing. "Why do you trail us?"

"A matter of theft. No man is pleased to be robbed."

"Robbed?"

"Yes—of gold rightfully mine."

"There was no robbery. We took only the amount that was ours—"

"Perhaps such is true where you are concerned. It is not so with your companion."

Sutton drew himself up sharply and wheeled to face Ben Gerlay. The deputy's eyes were on Torrero, a half-smile on his lips.

"In the pouch was more than one thousand dollars, gold—American money and Mexican *reales*. All was taken."

Anger boiled through Sutton; he was not beset by enough problems—Ben Gerlay had to continually create more.

He glared at the deputy. "That the truth?"

Gerlay laughed. "Sure—I took it. Why not? Figured we had it coming after what he done to us."

"We?"

"Well—I was going to tell you about it—split with you when I got the chance."

"Give it back."

The deputy's head came up. "Now, hold on—"

"Give it to him!" Jack Sutton's voice was cold as winter's wind.

Gerlay stared at the lawman's rigid shape for a long minute. Up on the slope one of the soldiers cocked his weapon, the click overloud in the tense quiet. Abruptly Gerlay's shoulders sagged in a gesture of resignation. He reached inside his shirt and withdrew a sack improvised from a handkerchief.

"Get what's yours," Jack ordered.

The deputy untied the knot and counted out forty-six dollars, which he thrust into his pocket. Retying the square of cloth, he tossed it to Torrero.

The captain caught the bag and nodded. "It is good we have no trouble. Nevertheless, a report to my government on the matter will be necessary."

"It would not be wise," Sutton countered. "You will

find difficulty in explaining your presence here. I also can make a report."

Torrero stirred uneasily in his saddle. "Perhaps it will be well to drop the matter. It is agreeable to me, if to you."

"Agreed," Sutton snapped. "Now—pull out! You've got your gold—"

The sharp, spiteful crack of a rifle cut through Jack's words. One of the soldiers on the slope cried out and fell forward, his weapon clattering noisily among the rocks. Wild yells crowded the gun's echo, and then more rifles began to speak.

"Apaches!" Ben Gerlay shouted and made a run for his horse.

A rider wheeled in beyond Torrero, firing a pistol at the officer. He wore the broad hat and silver trappings of a *vaquero*.

"They are not Indians!" the *commandante* yelled, spurring into the wash. "It is an old enemy—the bandit Ruiz. He has followed me."

Sutton swore, snapped a shot at the now retreating *vaquero*. Riders surged across the mouth of the arroyo, crouched low, shooting as they raced by. Torrero flinched but stayed on the saddle, firing with cool regularity. From the slope the second soldier was giving his support.

Backed against the low wall of the wash, Jack calculated his chances for reaching the bay. The horse was thirty feet distant and to reach him he must dare open ground, offer an easy target for the outlaws. Yet to remain in the wash was to die in a trap.

He emptied his pistol at the shadowy figures beyond the mouth of the arroyo and saw one fall, another sag and pull back. Hurriedly, he reloaded and then, crouched low, darted for the yonder side of the wash.

Bullets spurted sand around his feet, and once he felt a tug at his sleeve, but he reached the bay unharmed. Jerking loose the reins, he vaulted into the saddle.

Ben Gerlay, on the sorrel, was near the end of the arroyo, whipping back and forth as he fired at the indistinct shapes weaving in and out of the smoke and dust pall. Sutton cut in beside him, adding his direct shooting to that of the deputy and Juan Torrero.

At that moment the *rurale,* who had been in the higher rocks, came in from the opposite side, his pistol blasting. He had doubled back off the slope, obtained his horse and moved to side his *commandante.*

The attackers faltered, apparently believing reinforcements had arrived. The shooting fell off as the outlaws began to melt into the shadows along the base of the mountain, leaving several unmoving forms near the mouth of the wash.

"It is time for retreat!" Torrero said in a taut voice. He spurred to the side of his soldier. "What of Griego?"

"Dead, Captain. A bullet through the heart."

"Ben!" Sutton called. "You all right?"

The deputy's reply was low. "Sure."

Jack turned, threw a brief glance at the *rurale* officer, and crossed to where Gerlay waited. "Let's get out of here," he said, and urged the bay to a fast trot.

The deputy forged abreast. "What about the Mex?"

"His problem," Sutton replied. "Got my own."

XIII

THEY REACHED TUCSON IN THE EARLY MORNING hours, and found it still in darkness. Halting at the edge of town, Sutton studied the dim, sun-faded buildings.

"About that gold of Torrero's—" Gerlay began hesitantly. It was the first mention of it since Jack had compelled him to return it. "I was going to—"

"Forget it," Sutton cut in. "You pulling that stunt damn near got us killed—but it's done with now. I'm interested in one thing—finding Stinger Jones."

The deputy studied him quietly in the half dark. After a time, he said: "A man ever get away from you, Marshal?"

"Not yet. . . . Any idea where Stinger might hole up?"

"Nope. That whore in Nogales said he had a woman up here. Can't recollect her mentioning a name."

"She didn't. Guess a livery stable's the best place to start."

"Saloon would be good, too," the deputy said, regretfully. "Only there ain't none open."

"We'll try them later if we don't turn up something

at the stables," Jack said, moving on.

They located a livery barn almost immediately and turned toward its wide doors, both of which had been propped open to admit the slight breeze. Halting just inside, they dismounted. Gerlay crossed to a small room to their left which was used as an office. A boy with the fine, chiseled features of a Spaniard was sleeping in a chair, feet on a dust covered table. The deputy shook him awake and retraced his steps to the runway. The boy followed, yawning broadly.

"Take care of the horses," Gerlay ordered. "There a place around here where we can eat?"

The young hostler moved his head. "It is too early— all are closed. With sunrise—"

"Never mind that," Sutton broke in impatiently. "A man of the name Stinger Jones—do you know him? He wears a knife scar on his face."

The boy shook his head. "This man I have not seen."

"He came from Nogales two days ago . . . perhaps one. Think hard, it is likely he would have stabled his horse here."

The hostler shrugged. "There are other stables. Do you know the horse?"

Sutton and Gerlay had no idea of what the outlaw rode. The deputy said, "Any strangers come in?"

"Only you. There is not much business."

Sutton gave it up. It was obvious the boy knew nothing. He reached into his pocket for a silver dollar, tossed it to him.

"Grain, and a small amount of water for the horses.

Leave the gear on—it is possible we will leave in a hurry."

Grinning the boy led the bay and the sorrel off into the murky depths of the barn. Jack, with the deputy beside him, returned to the street.

Walking through the ankle deep dust, they pointed for the center of town. In the gray light the buildings all appeared vacant, the settlement deserted. Sutton noted a restaurant sign, halted and peered through the streaky glass of the window. He could see tables and chairs, a short counter; there were jars and cans on the shelves. Apparently it was a going concern.

"Nothing we can do until the town wakes up," he said, leaning against the wall of the structure. "Might as well wait here until this place opens. We can grab a bite to eat and then start looking for Stinger."

They were still there when the proprietor appeared an hour later. He eyed them with interest as he dug into his pockets for a key.

"You boys wanting to eat?"

Gerlay said, "Sure are. How long'll it take to fix us up?"

"Not long," the café man replied. "Come on in. Got some last night's coffee I can warm over. You can work on that while I throw some bacon on the stove."

The reheated coffee was strong, bitter. It was like a slug of whiskey on an empty stomach. Jack Sutton, sitting at a table with Gerlay, settled back in his chair, and gazed down the street of the slowly awakening town.

He thought of Billy, of Eduardo Bernal and the red scarf the Yaqui had been wearing, of Celestino—and all the other poor devils at the Mariposa; he'd do his best to bring an end to their suffering. He wondered then about Juan Torrero—if he had been able to escape his old enemy, Ruiz. Most likely he had; the Torrero's of the world always seemed to manage, somehow.

"Looking for a friend, name of Stinger Jones."

Vaguely he heard the deputy ask his question, and turned to hear the answer.

The café man paused over his stove. "Jones? Lot of Joneses around. Don't recollect one called Stinger."

"Short, a bit heavy. Got a big scar on his face."

"I see. What's he do?"

"Not much of anything, likely. Heard he'd come to Tucson just lately."

The man resumed his task of laying thick strips of bacon on the griddle. "Nope, don't think I know your Jones. If it's important, you might try asking a few other places—town's growing so's I don't know everybody any more."

The possibility that Stinger wasn't in Tucson pricked subtly at Jack Sutton's mind again, turning him dark and brooding. All he had to go on was the word of a drunken woman. She could have mentioned Tucson just to rid herself of his presence, or promote a fresh bottle of whiskey. And she could have heard wrong. In the condition she was in, very little would have registered correctly on her befuddled brain.

But it was the only lead he had—and one that must be followed. If it turned out the outlaw was not in Tucson, had not been there at all, in fact, then there would be nothing left to do but start back-tracking. He'd send Gerlay on to Trailbreak first, however.

The bacon started to sizzle and filled the room with its appetizing odor. Ben Gerlay said, "Don't have a couple of eggs you could put with that, do you?"

"Sure do. You both want 'em?"

Sutton nodded absently. Best plan to follow would be for the deputy and him to split up, each taking a side of the street. They should go from door to door asking for Stinger; if the outlaw were in town someone along the way would have seen him, perhaps even know where he could be found. The law of averages was sure to—

"Here y'are," the café man announced, breaking into his thoughts. "Fresh coffee's ready, too," he added, setting the platter of meat, eggs and hot biscuits before them. "Just dive in, boys. And if there ain't enough there, sing out. Got plenty more."

While they ate Jack explained his plan to Ben Gerlay. The deputy agreed that it was the only logical way to conduct the search but suggested that, if and when the outlaw was located, they both move in on him together: Stinger was a dangerous man. Sutton agreed, and when they had finished their meal and paid off, they returned to the street.

"Meet at the livery barn when we're through," Jack said as Gerlay started for the row of buildings opposite.

The deputy nodded and continued on. Sutton wheeled to the frame structure adjoining the restaurant, stepped up onto its narrow porch, and entered. It was a ladies clothing and dressmaking shop. He halted in the center of the room, hat in hand. It was unlikely anyone there would be acquainted with Stinger Jones, but the question had to be asked.

He was right. The elderly woman who came from the rear was startled at first by Jack's grizzled and trail-stained appearance, but she recovered enough to say she had never heard of a Stinger Jones or seen a man of his description. She advised Sutton to try the hotel. He thanked her and retraced his steps to the street. The hotel, he noted, was on a ways and on Gerlay's side. The deputy would be checking there.

His next stop was a general merchandise store. The owner, a short, balding man wearing steel rimmed spectacles, thought he might have seen Jones but wasn't sure. He proposed Sutton inquire at the Montezuma—the town's largest saloon. Most men eventually dropped by there, he said. There was gambling and dance girls as well as good liquor.

Jack agreed it was a promising possibility, and then realizing where he was, he reached into his pocket for some change.

"Need a little trail grub: coffee beans, hard biscuits, dry meat—the whole works. Lost my stock a few days back."

The groceryman nodded. "How much you want?"

"Leave it up to you—expect you know what a man

149

ought to have in his saddlebags."

The balding man smiled proudly. "Reckon I do. Been outfitting pilgrims for nine years or better. Couple of dollars'll cover it. If there's any change, you'll get it."

"Keep it. Be obliged if you'll send the order down to the livery barn at the edge of town—"

"Carabajal's?"

"Guess that's it. Tell the boy to put the stuff in the saddlebags on the bay that came in early this morning."

"Do just that," the merchant said, and began assembling the items.

The building adjoining the general store proved to be a dealer in feed. No, he had not seen a stranger answering to the name of Stinger Jones; no, there'd been nobody around his place who filled the description. Try the Montezuma.

Back on the wooden sidewalk Jack Sutton paused, scratched at the thick stubble covering the lower part of his face. Gerlay was nowhere in sight, evidently being in one of the stores at that moment. He looked for the Montezuma. It was further down, on his side of the street, a tall-fronted building ornately decorated with red and gold paint. He glanced at the window of the next shop.

THE GREAT WESTERN GUN CO.
New & Used Weapons
Expert Repairing
Peter Anson, Prop.

Jack crossed the canopied porch and entered the narrow room. The walls were lined with racks partly filled with rifles and shotguns; a glass showcase along one side contained revolvers and other types of hand weapons.

An elderly man rose from behind a workbench at the end of the room. "Yes, sir," he greeted, pushing a green eyeshade to the top of his head. "What can I do for you?"

"Looking for a fellow," Sutton replied, blunt and to the point. "Scarfaced—short and heavy. Goes by the name of Stinger Jones."

Anson returned Sutton's close study with a level gaze. "You a lawman?"

Jack felt his muscles tighten. The gunsmith knew something. "You see a badge on me?"

Anson shook his head, reached for his pipe and tobacco. Sutton leaned over the counter. "Know him?"

"Matter of fact, I do. Done some work for him only yesterday—Colts had a weak trigger spring."

Sutton drew himself up slowly as a mixture of relief and anticipation flowed through him. At last here was something definite.

"Any idea where he is now?"

"Over in his room, I suspect. Delivered his pistol to him there last night."

"Room? Where?"

"The hotel—No. 5. It's at the end of the hall."

Jack Sutton wheeled. It was hard to believe he had finally caught up with Stinger—so many things had got in the way since Trailbreak. He glanced through the window. The hotel was almost directly opposite.

"Early as it is, he ought to still be in his room," Anson said. "You see him, ask him how he likes the job I done."

Sutton nodded, said "Obliged to you," and stepped out onto the gallery.

He halted there, unconsciously touching the butt of his pistol as his eyes swept the sidewalk on the opposite side. The day's heat was clamping down and a dry wind was stirring dust in the street into small pinwheels. Ben Gerlay was still not in sight. Likely the deputy was inside the Mustanger Saloon, a place back a few doors, having himself a drink.

Sutton thought of Gerlay's suggestion that they move together against Jones when the moment came and debated its wisdom. It was a good idea, but he was reluctant to delay; five minutes spent in waiting for the deputy could be the five minutes in which the outlaw made an escape. And after all, Stinger Jones was just one man. Stepping off the gunsmith's porch, Jack crossed to the hotel and entered.

Halting in the small, stuffy lobby, he allowed his eyes to adjust. Directly ahead was the desk. There was no clerk; it was of no consequence for according to Anson, Stinger Jones occupied room No. 5, at the end of the hall. He shifted his glance to the left, located the corridor.

Drawing his pistol, he checked its loads, and keeping it in hand, walked softly down the dark, narrow hallway. A door facing him at its termination bore the crudely painted numeral 5.

He halted again, framing an answer to the question Jones would call out when he knocked. He considered. There was a chance the door wouldn't be locked—an off chance, but worth trying. He reached for the china knob, but checked himself abruptly.

Harsh, muffled words, the tones disturbingly familiar, came to him from inside the room.

"Don't tell me that—you double-crossing sonofabitch! I know better!"

It was Ben Gerlay's voice.

XIV

JACK SUTTON FROZE INTO IMMOBILITY, STUNNED BY the implication of the deputy's words: Gerlay had been a party to the robbery and killings, a shadow in the background, not physically participating, but aiding in a way that only a trusted lawman could.

And all the while, all those days and nights, he had let Jack keep going—searching, sweating out the hours while the noose drew tighter around Billy's neck.

A haze began to fill Jack Sutton's eyes, to cloud his mind with a burning hate. Ben Gerlay wanted to reach Stinger Jones first—had to, actually; he must silence the outlaw before he could speak and lay the whole

153

sorry deal in the open. Billy had been a fortunate coincidence for them, riding in when he did, and Ben Gerlay had been quick to take advantage of the opportunity and unload the blame. Likely the deputy figured the people of Trailbreak would be satisfied with one man to hang from their scaffold and they'd stop looking for the others.

But he hadn't figured on Billy's brother coming into the picture, disputing the evidence and starting a search for the men who really committed the crimes. Thus Gerlay, to protect himself, had volunteered to go along—not to aid as he had professed, but to prevent the capture of the outlaws.

It was ironic, Jack Sutton thought; he had pursued Stinger Jones and Joe Harp to arrest them and make them talk; Ben Gerlay had ridden at his side to keep that very thing from taking place.

"Wasn't aiming to cheat you, Ben," Jones' voice had assumed a desperate note. "Before God, I wasn't!"

"Not much! You'll be telling me next you didn't fix it with that Mex *commandante* to sell me to that goddam mining outfit!"

"Didn't know he was doing that—"

"Like hell you didn't! Same as told us. . . . Where's the money?"

"Saddlebags—there in the closet. Go ahead, take your share, if you ain't trusting me no more. Hell, I was on my way to Silver City, just like we planned so's we could divvy up. That's the God's truth, Ben— You know it. We been friends a long time—"

"Not no more," Gerlay's words were a promise—a threat.

Jack Sutton had heard enough. He reached for the knob a second time. The hall echoed dully from a blast inside the room. Fear welled through Sutton—fear that he had waited too long—that his one hope of clearing Billy had ended in an exchange of bullets.

He forgot the knob, and hurled himself against the door. The panel splintered, burst open. Off balance, he stumbled into the room. He had a quick glimpse of Stinger Jones sprawled across the bed, of Ben Gerlay, saddlebags over his shoulder, pistol in hand—wheeling to face him.

The deputy fired even as he spun. Shock jolted Sutton's arm as his revolver was torn from his grasp. His senses reeled as the hurtling weapon struck him a glancing blow on the temple. He went to his knees, clinging to consciousness, dimly aware of Ben Gerlay climbing through the window.

He hung there on hands and knees, pain raking him, vision swimming in sickening circles. He shook himself violently. Gradually his head began to clear. Faint shouts, coming from the street or possibly the lobby of the hotel, penetrated the numbness. He dragged himself upright by clinging to the end of the bed. Stinger Jones groaned weakly.

Sutton shook himself again, savagely, striving to dispel the effects of the blow his own pistol, smashed against his head by the deputy's lucky shot, had caused. His mind was functioning only partly; all things seemed behind a filmy curtain of cobwebs. Uncertainly, he crossed to the window. The deep draughts of hot, fresh air helped.

He could hear men shouting questions in the street, but the passageway below the window was empty. He turned then, to glance toward the door. There was no one in the hall. Apparently the source of the gunshots was still unknown.

His brain clearing rapidly now, he looked again into the passageway. Gerlay was gone, of course, but he knew where the deputy would be heading—straight for the stable and his horse. Likely he was not too afraid of immediate pursuit; he would think Sutton dead along with Stinger Jones. It would be in his mind to leave town quickly but without attracting undue attention.

Jones—

Sutton wheeled to the bed. He must know for sure about Billy. He must hear it from the outlaw's own lips. Leaning over, he shook the man roughly.

"Stinger! Listen to me!"

The outlaw opened his eyes and struggled to settle them on Jack. "Who—who're you?"

"Name's Sutton. I'm a U.S. Marshal. They're holding a boy back in Trailbreak—claim he was a part of your gang. Name's Billy."

"Who?"

"Billy! Was he in on the bank robbery?"

"Billy?" Stinger Jones' eyes rolled helplessly. "Ben—shot me—Marshal. Ben Gerlay—"

"I know that—and I'll get him. What about the boy—man—Billy?"

Stinger shuddered, closed his lips. Sutton gripped him by the arms, pulled him half up.

"Talk—damn you! Hear me, Stinger? You're dying! If you don't tell me the truth, Billy'll hang for something he didn't do!"

"Billy," the outlaw echoed vacantly, not opening his eyes. "Don't—know Billy. Was me—and Harp—Jesse—and Ben and—"

"There wasn't a man called Billy mixed up with you in it?"

"Don't—know Billy—"

Jack Sutton released his grip of the outlaw, allowing him to sink back. Satisfaction trickled through him—Billy was innocent, as he had known all the time. Next move was to catch up with Ben Gerlay, take him back to Trailbreak and make him confess. It shouldn't be hard to do; the deputy thought him dead.

He turned, hearing a sound at the splintered door. Several men stood in the opening, one of them a lawman.

"Stand easy, mister. Sheriff'll be here in a couple of minutes."

Sutton pointed to the shattered pistol on the floor. "What the hell's the matter with you, deputy? I didn't do the shooting. Man who did got away through that window after taking a shot at me."

The deputy picked up the useless gun and examined it carefully. "Busted all to pieces," he observed,

157

handing it to the man beside him. "You know who the killer is?"

"I do, and I'm going after him."

The young lawman frowned. "Expect you'd better wait for the sheriff."

It wouldn't do to let Gerlay get too long a start. Abruptly Jack pushed by the deputy, allowing him no moment for further protest, and shouldered his way through the men.

"No time for that. Name's Sutton—I'm a U.S. Marshal. Sheriff can check me in the records if he likes. I'll be at Carabajal's stables, getting my horse."

Grim faced, he walked hurriedly down the hall into the lobby and out to the street. He wasted no time on caution when he reached the stable. Gerlay would not be hiding there; he would be putting distance between himself and Tucson. He might feel secure in that he believed no witness to the shootings in the hotel was alive—but he was too smart to press his luck.

A man in dirty overalls came out of the stable office, to meet Jack in the runway. He halted, hands thrust deep in his pockets.

"Looking for something?"

"My horse," Sutton snapped. "Bay—with the saddle still on him."

The man nodded. "Be a dollar—"

"Paid this morning—" Jack began and dropped it. Arguing would take time, and it wasn't worth the effort. He dug out the necessary coin and flipped it to the hostler who turned, moving off with aggravating slowness.

"You been here all morning?" Jack asked when the man reappeared leading the bay.

"Reckon I have. . . . My job."

Sutton made a hasty check of his gear. Everything was in place. "Man with a sorrel—probably came for him a few minutes ago—which way did he head out?"

The hostler hung his thumbs in the bib of his overalls, rocked back on his heels. "Well, now, don't know as that's any of your business—"

Anger swept through Jack Sutton in a sudden gale. He pivoted, seized the man's shirt front, whirled him about and slammed him hard against the wall of the office.

"Goddam you—I've got no time to waste! Talk up—or I'll knock your brains out!"

The hostler's arrogance fled swiftly. He gulped, then pointed at the door. "Went north."

Jack shoved the man aside, and wheeled to the bay. He stepped to the saddle. Temper still flowing through him, he looked down at the hostler. "That better be the truth."

"It is—so help me!"

Sutton nodded curtly and rode down the runway into the street. North was the logical direction for the deputy to follow.

XV

GERLAY WILL NEVER LET ME TAKE HIM ALIVE, JACK Sutton thought as he swung north onto the dusty road. He knows there'll be a rope waiting for him—and when I close in, he'll make a stand and gamble on shooting it out with me. I'll have to kill him—or be killed. And I need him alive, otherwise Billy will hang for sure.

He looked ahead. The deputy, at most, could have no more than a half hour lead. It would be wise to let him think no one was on his trail—at least until he had passed the Catalinas lying to the northeast of the settlement. If Gerlay got suspicious and sought a hiding place in the rugged mountains, it would take all hell to root him out. Anyway, as long as he continued north, in the general direction of Trailbreak, let him ride, let him go. .

Mopping at the sweat on his face, Sutton glanced at the glaring sun. The heat was rapidly reaching its worst; shimmering layers hung above the baked sand and even the pale green of mesquite clumps appeared a washed-out gray. Overhead the sky was a clean, clear blue with only a scattering of feathery clouds hovering about the Tortolitos on to the north.

Jack got his first glimpse of the fleeing deputy shortly before noon, and that was only of a dim figure moving slowly along in the center of a dust boil. Immediately Sutton abandoned the road in favor of a position parallel and to the side. If Gerlay chose to check the trail behind him, he would find no one in sight.

What would he do if Gerlay decided to swing west or otherwise deviate from his northerly course? Jack considered that, again realizing the deputy would fight rather than surrender. Jack couldn't put up much of a shootout anyway, he remembered suddenly; he had not taken time to replace the revolver the deputy had ruined. He had only his rifle.

The rifle. . . .

Immediately a thought claimed Jack Sutton's mind. The long gun could be the answer. With it he could remain at a distance, beyond pistol range, and force—literally drive—Gerlay to do his bidding. It meant constant vigilance, but he would manage that somehow; the point was that he had a means of compelling the deputy to do as he ordered and still avoid a shootout. Sutton smiled grimly. He now had the answer.

He wondered where the deputy intended to go. There was little of consequence in the direction he was following except small settlements that would hold no attractions for a man of Gerlay's newfound wealth. He could have it in his head to push on to Denver—perhaps even to the Dakotas. Things were humming there.

But Ben Gerlay would never see any of that country:

Jack'd let the deputy get as far as the Gila River, which lay west of Trailbreak, and then move in to start hazing him eastward across the Natanes Plateau, through the Mogollons, and on to the settlement.

He'd make it rough on Gerlay, not give him any rest or allow him to stop for food. He had the advantage there; the deputy had only a canteen while he was supplied both with water and grub. If he crowded the man hard enough, punishing and taunting him, Gerlay might give in and surrender before they reached the Mogollons, or at least the San Mateos beyond.

Early in the afternoon, with the heat now a fierce, murderous enemy, Jack Sutton reached the upper end of the Catalinas. He swung wide to the west, not certain if Gerlay paused at the tip of the range or not. Minutes later he saw the deputy had chosen to keep moving and was now angling east. Most likely he intended to camp that night along the San Pedro River. Sutton grinned. It fit nicely with his plan.

Gerlay arrived at the San Pedro near sundown. He was too distant for Sutton to note his exact movements, but he did halt, dismount. Jack waited until full dark and then rode in as near as he dared, pulling the bay to a stop in a deep wash a quarter mile or so west of the deputy.

He lay on the rim of the ravine and waited until Gerlay, apparently to dispel the loneliness of a solitary camp, built a small fire and settled down. Jack then unsaddled the bay, gave him a little water and picketed him to a squat cedar under which a few blades of grass struggled to survive.

Sutton made a meal for himself of biscuits and tinned peaches, avoiding a fire over which he could have made coffee. In the wash, well below the horizon, a small flame probably would not have been noticeable, but there could be a glare and he refused to accept the risk.

He wished Gerlay would use some caution. The deputy had no actual need for a fire since he had nothing to cook, and a light in the night, however small, was a beacon prowling Apaches could not resist. He recalled mentioning such danger to the deputy; either the man had forgotten the warning or was arbitrarily ignoring it.

Sutton kept himself awake well after midnight, his eyes on Gerlay, but weariness finally overran him and he dropped off to sleep. He awoke with a start a few hours later, and looked anxiously toward the deputy's camp. In the first pearly light of the new day he could distinguish the outlines of the big red sorrel. Relieved, Jack lay back. He had not intended to sleep for any length of time; Gerlay could have decided to move on during the night. That would be his worst problem, he realized, once he closed in on the deputy—staying awake.

He ate of his stock of food, saddled the bay and sat back to await Ben Gerlay's next move. It was not long in coming. At sunup the deputy mounted the sorrel and struck off. For several moments he was visible, and then he disappeared briefly while he forded the San Pedro, to again come into view on the opposite bank. Sutton allowed him to get on his way, pulled out of the wash, and maintaining his parallel course, resumed the pursuit.

Gerlay continued north while Sutton, a silent shadow in the distance, kept pace. It became apparent that the deputy was going to cross the vast Natanes flat along the western edge. Unwittingly, he was playing into Jack's hands. By nightfall the deputy would have reached a position approximately due west of Trailbreak. It would be time to take over the task of pushing him eastward that following morning.

They forded the Gila, belly deep to the horses, late in the morning and by mid-afternoon were well up on the slopes of the hills that fringed the plateau. There was more cover available now and Sutton shortened the gap that separated him from his ward. Although it was some cooler, he saw Gerlay take frequent turns at his canteen. Hunger likely was gnawing at the man by that hour and he was endeavoring to still the pains with water.

At dark when Gerlay finally halted, they were on the Natanes.

Jack Sutton watched the deputy prepare for the night, aware that hunger was making the job that lay ahead easier with each passing minute. Given another foodless day and Gerlay, conceivably, would be ready to talk terms. But that day would be one of critical import—one in which Jack would have to bend the deputy to his will by sheer threat while affording the man no opportunity to fight back.

Well before sunrise Sutton was up and about. He saddled the bay, had a hurried breakfast, and then checked the magazine of his rifle. Finding it fully loaded, he moved in behind a thick shoulder of rock from which he could look down upon Gerlay.

The deputy slept, a prone, undisturbed shape near the blackened ashes of his fire. Near him lay his canteen. Sutton took close aim on the container, then pressed off a shot. The canteen leaped from the ground and slammed to one side at the bullet's impact. Gerlay sat bolt upright, hand clawing for his pistol as he looked wildly around. A few paces away the tall sorrel fought his lines in fright.

Sutton waited until the echoes died, and then cupping his hands to his lips, shouted: "Gerlay!"

The deputy came to his feet. Crouched, he probed the surrounding area with quick, darting glances.

"Marshal—that you?"

From his place of concealment Jack answered. "It's me. . . . Been on your trail ever since Tucson."

Ben Gerlay's voice betrayed his shock. "I—I thought—"

"Figured wrong, Ben, I'm plenty alive . . . and I'm taking you to Trailbreak."

The deputy stiffened. "Like hell you are!"

"Stinger told me everything before he died. You're going to clear my brother."

"I ain't doing nothing—"

165

"You'll go. I aim to drive you every foot of the way if I have to."

"Drive me? I'd like to see that. . . ."

"You will. Move out now—due east. Take one step in any other direction—and I'll crack down on you with my rifle. First time will be the warning to turn back—second time I'll put a bullet in you."

"You won't do that," the deputy yelled with a show of confidence. "I ain't no good to you dead."

"Maybe—but a slug in your leg—or your arm—won't kill you straight off. . . . Might die later of blood poisoning—but I'd get you to Trailbreak in time. You ever try riding across country like this—day after day—with a bullet in you, deputy? Pure hell. . . ."

Gerlay was silent for a long minute. Then, "Guess you got the top hand, Marshal. Come on in, let's talk this thing over."

"Not a chance. I'm not letting you crowd me into a gunfight where I'd have to kill you to keep myself alive. I'll stay like I am—out of pistol range but close enough to where my rifle can make you toe the mark."

"You're crazy!" Gerlay shouted in a wild burst of exasperation. "You can't—"

"I can—and I sure will," Sutton yelled back. "But I'll make it easy on you. Drop your gunbelt and take that pistol and throw it into the rocks. Then I'll come down and we'll ride together—be no sweat. I've got grub and water. . . . You're going to get plenty hungry before we reach town."

"I'll make out!" Gerlay replied with childish stubbornness. "And you got another guess coming if you think you can make me do something I don't want—"

He rushed for the sorrel. Midway he noticed the ruined canteen, and paused to pick it up as though hoping it would still be of use. He glanced at it, flung it angrily into the brush, and strode on.

Sutton turned to the bay and swung aboard, keeping behind the rocky shoulder. He knew he was beyond reach of the deputy's pistol and that the concealment was unnecessary, but the very fact that he could not be seen was unnerving to Ben Gerlay.

The deputy, uncertain as to what he could do, took considerable time tightening the gear of the sorrel. Finally he went to the saddle. Casting a furtive glance over his shoulder, he deliberately moved forward resuming the northerly course he had been following.

Jack lifted his rifle, drove a shot into the ground immediately in front of the red horse. The sorrel went to his hind legs in sudden fright.

"Next one draws blood!" Sutton warned.

Gerlay fought his horse until he was again calm, and then wheeled to face Jack. It was still only half light and considerable distance separated them but Sutton could see the black anger that tore at the deputy's features.

"Goddam you, Sutton! You're not getting away with this! You can't make me do nothing—my chance'll come, you'll see!"

Jack sighed, settling back. It had been easier than he had expected. "Head east!" he shouted. "And keep remembering—I'm watching every move you make!"

"Soon's it's dark—it'll be another story—"

"Won't make any difference, Ben. You'll never get out from under my rifle. You're on your way to Trailbreak. . . . Whether you get there in one piece or dripping blood's up to you."

"You can't keep watching all night. You got to sleep."

"I can stay awake long enough to break you. After that I won't worry about it."

"Break?"

"Sure—a man's got to eat and drink, and the next creek's a long ride from here. Could be we'll find it dry, like the Carretas was. Man goes out of his head when his belly's empty and his tongue swells up to where it's choking him. . . ."

"Gone hungry before. And thirsty. I can stand it."

"Won't be the same. . . . You'll have this rifle looking at you day and night. Every time you move, I'll be ready to shoot. Maybe it'll be in the leg . . . or the arm. Could be the shoulder bone. I'll be a little jumpy, too. Might just make a mistake—shoot when I wasn't supposed to. . . ."

Ben Gerlay, head slumped forward on his chest, considered in silence.

"Better take my offer," Jack yelled, his voice beginning to hoarsen from the shouting. "Throw away your pistol and we'll ride together. You'll eat and drink, and there won't be no chance for me to make a bad mistake."

The deputy looked up abruptly. "Go to hell!" he answered and wheeled the sorrel around savagely.

But he moved off into the face of the rising sun.

XVI

Jack Sutton had no problems with the deputy that day while they were crossing the high, wild flat known as the Natanes Plateau. It was clear Gerlay was biding his time until darkness fell when he would put some plan he had conceived into operation. It would be a hard night, Jack realized, one during which he must be alert every moment. In preparation for it he dozed when he could as the bay plodded steadily on.

They were approximately two-thirds of the way across the broad tableland when night came. Jack allowed Gerlay to pick his own camp, a small coulee around which the brush grew thick, and chose for himself a position somewhat higher. From that elevated point he would have no difficulty in observing the deputy's activities, and while well beyond revolver range, it was within the rifle's effective distance.

He built himself a fire, and using the empty peach can saved from a previous meal, boiled up some coffee, noting with perverse satisfaction that the light breeze carried the odor down to the deputy. He had no spider in his equipment and had to roast the strips of already dried meat over the open flames. Ben Gerlay became aware also of that good smell.

When darkness closed in, Sutton had completed his chores and settled down in the rocks to watch his prisoner.

Gerlay seemed content to simply rest, making a bed of leaves and small branches torn from the nearby brush, and taking elaborate pains to arrange a comfortable pallet; he built no fire. The evening wore on. Sutton brewed a second tin of coffee. The moon broke through a thin overcast, spread weak light across the land, but it was sufficient to illuminate the area. . . . Somewhere close by a mountain lion pierced the hush with its peculiar woman-like scream.

Near midnight Jack saw Gerlay stir, sit up slowly, and turn his face toward the rocks. The deputy studied the shadowy point where Sutton lay for several minutes. He got to his feet, finally. Again he paused to stare. Jack grinned bleakly. Gerlay believed him to be asleep.

Quietly Sutton brought his rifle to bear on the man, muffling the click of the hammer by cupping his hand over it. Gerlay took a tentative step toward the rocks, halted. He stalled out a full minute, then drawing his pistol, crept forward.

The night rocked with the rifle's blast. Dust and litter spewed over Gerlay's feet. He yelled, leaped back, mouthing curses.

"Go back to bed," Sutton drawled from the rocks.

The deputy whirled angrily, jammed the pistol into its holster and returned to his pallet. Stretching out, he removed his hat and tipped it over his eyes.

Sutton considered the man thoughtfully. It was nothing short of cruelty to put him through such torture, but to him Ben Gerlay deserved no better. That he not only dishonored the badge he wore, but could stand by and see an innocent man dragged to the gallows for a crime in which he, personally, was involved, placed him in a category reserved only for the lowest form of life.

Added to that, he was a cold-blooded killer, as he had proved in Tucson. He warranted no mercy—and he would pay for his guilt; he would hang on that scaffold built for Billy Sutton, and the world would be better off for his passing.

Three hours later Ben Gerlay saw fit to make a second try for freedom. It was short lived. Jack watched him sit up, again doing so slowly, and then rise to his feet.

"Forget it, Ben!" Sutton yelled through the hush. "Won't get as far as you did last time. . . ."

The deputy relaxed, made no further attempts. Jack, following his preconceived plan, prepared the bay, ate his meal well before sunrise, and then with deliberate intention, awoke Gerlay with a rifle bullet placed near his head.

The deputy, shocked and trembling, lunged to his feet screaming curses and threats as he stared at the rocks in which Jack had made camp. Finally, anger spent, he calmed.

"Mount up," Sutton shouted. "I'm pressed for

time—want to reach the New Mexico border by dark."

"You won't make it—"

Sutton drove a second rifle bullet into the ground between the man's feet. The deputy jumped, and shaking with helpless rage, saddled the sorrel and climbed aboard.

"Four more days of this . . ." Jack reminded him. "Better take my offer."

Gerlay turned, gave Sutton a hating stare, and moved on without answering.

The hours passed, hot and seemingly endless. Jack, beginning to feel the heavy pressure of fatigue, fought to stay erect in the saddle, fearful now of resorting to brief naps that so far had sustained him. Ben Gerlay, sullen and morose, rode with head down, making no effort to break away. Sutton began to suspect that a new plan of escape was shaping up in the man's mind, and looked forward to the night with no relish.

They camped not far from the New Mexico line shortly after sundown, and as Sutton dismounted and began to make his nightly preparations, he again hoarsely shouted his conditions of surrender to the deputy.

Gerlay turned to face him, laughing in a high-pitched, unnerving way. "What's the matter, Marshal? You peterin' out? Four bits to a dime says I outlast you!"

Jack went ahead with his chores. He boiled up coffee, ate of his food supply, and got himself set for the coming hours. He had been unable to purloin any large amount of sleep during the day and his eyes were heavy.

This disturbed him and to offset the weariness, he kept the peach can filled with coffee, boiled to bitterness. Each time he felt the numbness of fatigue possessing him, he reached for the tin, and took a deep swallow to drive away the insidious webs.

They were yet three days from Trailbreak . . . three days and nights, counting the one he was presently enduring. He calculated his chances for completing the journey; they were slim, he was forced to admit—unless Ben Gerlay capitulated or forced him to use a crippling bullet.

He had expected the deputy to be weakening by the time they crossed the Natanes, but Gerlay had surprised him. It was the gold the deputy carried that was giving him unnatural strength and determination, Jack concluded.

Through sagging eyelids he studied the man, now sprawled on a grassy knoll, sleeping soundly. As the hours crept by and the first gray of the new day began to flare in the eastern sky, it became apparent to Sutton that Gerlay had not intended to try for an escape; the man was playing a game of his own now—one of nerves aimed at breaking down his captor. Jack shook his head. It was either that or the deputy was nearer total exhaustion than he figured.

He raised the rifle to fire the customary nerve shattering bullet that would awaken the deputy. Then he paused, lowering the weapon. Gerlay was sleeping the sleep of the utterly spent. Perhaps the opportunity he had hoped for, that of slipping up on the man and disarming him, was at hand. . . . It was worth a try.

Moving stealthily in the faint light, Sutton came from behind the screen of mountain mahogany where he had built camp. Wary, rifle ready for instant use, he crept toward the snoring deputy.

Abruptly Ben Gerlay leaped to his feet, revolver in hand. Sutton lunged to the side as the deputy fired twice in rapid succession. Both bullets were wild. Sutton, taking no further risk, doubled back to his position of concealment.

"Fooled you!" Gerlay shouted gleefully, his voice, a raspy croak. "Figured you'd be trying that. Was just waiting. Now who's running this here show?"

Sutton squinted at the deputy, tried hard for a look at his face. Ben Gerlay seemed to think he had assumed command, and was now free. Jack leveled the rifle and placed a bullet at the man's feet.

"Get your horse ready!" he ordered. "We're moving out."

Laughing Gerlay threw another shot in Sutton's general direction. Suddenly he sobered, seeming to recover his senses. He looked at the pistol in his hand for a full minute, then wagged his head slowly. Jack brought the rifle to bear again. If he could get a clean shot at Gerlay's weapon, he could bring matters under control quickly.

But it was a small, indefinite target, and only half

exposed to him. After a moment he lowered the long gun; Gerlay had turned further around, flipped open the loading gate of the pistol, and was methodically punching out the empty cartridges and replacing them. Then, jamming the weapon into its holster, he walked to the sorrel and began to throw on his gear.

Jack Sutton sighed. The opportunity had almost presented itself, but perhaps it would come again. He swung onto the bay and a few minutes later they were moving.

The day promised to be another hot one. Gerlay, Jack noted as they pressed on, seemed to become affected by the heat more than ordinarily. He continually pulled at his shirt front, loosening the garment; several times he removed his hat and mopped at his whiskered, haggard face and head.

Just before midday when they got their first sighting of the towering, pine clad Mogollons, the deputy elected to try his luck again. They were descending a long draw with Gerlay following the trail along its floor while Sutton, from a higher position, kept watch.

As if on impulse, Gerlay suddenly drove his heels into the sorrel's flanks and began to lash the horse with the trailing ends of the leathers. The red plunged forward, charging recklessly down the steep grade.

"Look out!" Sutton yelled, fearful of the horse falling.

Gerlay flogged his mount harder. Sutton hurried on, staying to the slight hogback. Raising his rifle, he waited until the sorrel had reached bottom, and then he squeezed off a shot at a rotting stump slightly ahead of the gelding.

As the rifle cracked, splintered wood and dust erupted in the sorrel's eyes. The horse swerved sharply, almost unseating Gerlay, and went to its knees. The deputy yelled, flung himself clear.

"You damn fool!" Sutton, furious, shouted down at him as the sorrel struggled to regain his four feet. "You could have broken that horse's legs! Try that again and I'll make you walk the rest of the way."

Gerlay pulled himself upright slowly. He faced Sutton, his eyes like colorless marbles buried deep in his head.

"When we stopping?" His words were so low, so spiritless, Jack could scarcely hear them.

"Not yet—keep going."

"I'm beat, got to rest . . ."

"You can last 'til dark."

"No . . . can't do it. Can't."

There was a lost quality to Ben Gerlay's cry. A tug of pity stirred Sutton, and then the old hatred brushed it ruthlessly aside.

"River's on ahead, hour or so. We'll camp there." He paused, added with small hope. "You ready to throw down your gun?"

Strength flowed back into the deputy at the question. He shook his head violently. "Hell no—I ain't!" he yelled, and climbing back onto the nervous sorrel, moved on.

They reached the San Francisco River at sunset.

Sutton waited, as uusal, while the deputy chose his spot, and then went about selecting a vantage point for himself, always keeping one eye on the man's movements.

He stiffened suddenly, seeing Gerlay abruptly draw his pistol and drop to his knees. Stepping to where he could see better, he watched the man inch his way toward a grassy hummock rising at one end of the swale in which he had halted. The deputy stopped, stretched out full length on his belly. He aimed the pistol carefully, holding it in both hands, and fired.

With a shout Ben Gerlay leaped to his feet and ran to the hummock. Reaching down, he picked up a rabbit. Still yelling, he spun, holding it aloft for Jack to see.

"Figured you'd starve me out, eh? Like hell. I fooled you. . . ."

He trotted back to the center of the swale, hastily kicked some twigs and dry branches into a pile and struck a fire. Alternately laughing and yelling, he skinned the animal and suspended it above the flames by use of a cross stick and two forked uprights.

Sutton watched the proceedings in silence, knowing what had to be done and feeling no compunction. He allowed the rabbit to roast until it smelled as though it were almost ready; then, taking careful aim, he blasted the small morsel into bits.

Gerlay leaped from a squatting position near the fire and began to dart erratically about. He screamed, the shrill sound evoking a chain of startled echoes that rocked off into the closing night. Suddenly he whirled and ran straight at Sutton, arms waving, mouth working grotesquely.

"Damn you, Sutton! Goddam your black soul to hell! I'm going to kill you—"

Jack halted him with a bullet that sprayed dirt over his feet. The deputy stood quiet, breathing heavily as he stared up the slope. After a time he began to wag his head from side to side.

"Ain't right—starving a man," he cried in a desperate voice. "Ain't right."

"You can end it," Sutton called back. "Throw that gun in the river, and you'll sleep with a full belly tonight."

The deputy continued to shake his head. "I ain't quitting. My time'll come."

"Not much time left."

"Enough," Gerlay said, and dropping to his hands and knees, began to search out the fragments of meat scattered around the fire.

Jack watched him briefly, then looked off to the west where a bank of low lying clouds were gradually losing their gold as the sun sank below the horizon. Tomorrow night they would be in the San Mateos, and that following day—Trailbreak.

Then it would all end. Billy would go free and Ben Gerlay would receive the punishment he merited. He guessed he'd take Billy with him: his brother wouldn't have any desire to remain in that part of the country now. He'd help Billy get a job around Denver. It

178

would be no problem: he had quite a few friends in that area.

Sutton glanced at Ben Gerlay. The deputy had scratched leaves into a bed, and now lay face down upon it. He appeared to be asleep. Jack stirred wearily; he'd give a lot for a night's sleep, but it was out of the question. He was too close now to take any risks.

He settled back and reached for the coffee. Only one more night after this one—and then nothing to worry about. He reckoned he'd just lie down and sleep for a week when that time finally came. . . .

XVII

THE FOLLOWING NIGHT AT THE FOOT OF THE SAN Mateos was the worst of all for Jack Sutton. He had gone so long without sufficient rest or complete sleep that his mind was languid, and functioned only when prodded by sudden emergency.

The day had been marked by tension and strain. They were passing through a land well timbered by pines, broad-based spruces and dense underbrush; there were times when Ben Gerlay was momentarily lost to Sutton's sight and he was compelled to move quickly else the man be afforded an opportunity for escape.

Fortunately, Gerlay was in even worse condition, if not from fatigue, from lack of food. He rode, as usual, head down, sullen, wholly withdrawn and paying no attention to anything that transpired. Once a spike deer leaped from his path and bounded off into the shadows but the deputy failed to note its passage. He was like a mindless, wooden man moving at the direction of his master.

Daylight of the final morning dawned with the threat of rain hanging over the glazed rocks of the mountains. Sutton, barely on his feet, prepared his tasteless breakfast, got the bay ready for riding and picked up his rifle to fire the shot that would awaken Gerlay.

He was surprised to find the deputy already up and sluggishly going about the chore of saddling and bridling the red gelding. Jack waited until the man had finished and again made his offer.

"Be in town by noon. Be smart—make the rest of the trip easy on yourself."

The deputy, weaving on his feet, gave him a brief, angry look and climbed stiffly onto his horse. He moved off immediately, not waiting for Sutton's command.

The rain held off and the hovering clouds served only to increase the oppressiveness of the heat as they worked slowly around the lower end of the range. Several times Jack saw Gerlay remove his hat, mop at his face and neck in a quick, nervous fashion. He was suffering deeply.

"Want to stop—rest?" he shouted. "There's shade under those cedars."

Immediately Gerlay pulled off the rutted road, and angled toward the cluster of small trees, hardly more than large bushes. He half fell from the sorrel, caught himself and hung there sagging against the horse for a time.

Finally he drew himself up, turned and staggered for the nearest of the trees. Sutton, off the bay, saw him halt unsteadily, take a half step backward. Sunlight glinted on his pistol as he drew suddenly. The canyons along the San Mateos came alive abruptly as he began firing rapidly, uncontrollably at something among the rocks.

The weapon snapped on an empty cartridge. The deputy continued to cock and pull the trigger, all the while yelling something Sutton could not distinguish. Unexpectedly he wheeled, and stared at the lawman.

"Goddam you!" he shrieked, and broke into a shambling run. "You want this here gun—take it!"

He rushed on, stumbling, half falling. His eyes were wild, his face distorted under its sweat and dust-clotted beard. His mouth opened and closed spasmodically as he gasped for air.

Sutton leaned his rifle against a clump of rabbit-brush and waited. Gerlay went down full length, scrambled upright, came on. . . .

"You ain't taking me in! Nobody makes me do something I don't want. . . . I got plenty money now—ain't nobody going to push me around. Hear?"

The jumbled torrent of words faltered as Gerlay's steps slowed. He sagged forward and fell to his knees.

Mustering his remaining strength, he threw the revolver at Sutton.

"Here's the goddam gun—" he shrilled, and collapsed into a dusty heap.

Jack Sutton stepped forward. Grasping the deputy under the armpits, he dragged him to the shelter of the cedars. Returning for his rifle and the bay, he led the horse to the side of the sorrel, and then unhooking his canteen, forced a little water into Ben Gerlay's throat and poured a bit more onto his face. After that he built a fire, made coffee and warmed food for the exhausted man.

Gerlay roused and ate mechanically, taking no particular interest in the meal. Only the coffee seemed to have effect but it failed also to dispel the vacant depths in his rimmed, bloodshot eyes. Yet, when he had finished, he looked at Jack Sutton and said, "One more day and I'd of got you, Marshal."

Jack paused. "Doubt that. You were ready to cave in yesterday."

"I'd of kept going," the deputy said stubbornly. He looked out over the yucca studded flat to the south. "Ain't far from town."

"Couple hours. . . . Ready?"

Gerlay rose, slanted an odd, sly glance at Sutton. "Sure, Marshal, I'm ready."

They reached the edge of Trailbreak a few minutes before high noon. A shout immediately went up at recognition of the two gaunt, bearded men, both of whom looked more dead than alive; by the time

Sutton had herded his prisoner up to the hitchrack fronting the courthouse, half the settlement had gathered.

Henry Parmalee and Sheriff McMasters came hurriedly from the interior of the building, both frowning. Sutton dismounted and moved to the sorrel. Reaching up, he took the deputy by the arm, pulled him off the saddle, and roughly shoved him at the two officials.

"Here's the man you want!" he croaked. "Now turn my brother loose."

No one spoke. Sutton glanced over the crowd, then stepped nearer to Parmalee and the sheriff.

"Gerlay was in it with Stinger Jones and the rest. They cooked up the bank robbery between them. Billy had nothing to do with it—Stinger told me that before he died. You'll find the money on the deputy."

Parmalee came off the landing. His face was taut and his lips were pulled to a thin, gray line.

"What the hell's wrong with you?" Sutton demanded angrily. "Gerlay'll talk—I'll make him if need be. He'll clear Billy."

Parmalee shook his head. "You—you don't understand, Marshal."

"Understand what? The outlaws are all dead—except Gerlay. You can try him for the killings—"

The judge turned and pointed to a weedy slope where a number of tombstones and weathered headboards perched drunkenly in the sandy soil.

"I can't turn Billy loose. . . . He's over there. Was hung a week ago. . . ."

Jack Sutton staggered as though he had been struck. Gerlay began to laugh senselessly.

"Hung!" Jack shouted hoarsely. "Why—in God's name? You got my letter—you should have waited. . . ."

"Letter?" Parmalee echoed. "What letter?"

"One I sent you from Nogales. It told you about Harp—why I'd been delayed. Said we were moving in on Stinger—"

Sutton's words trailed off. He turned slowly to face Ben Gerlay as understanding came to him. "You—you sonofabitch! You never posted that letter—you tore it up!"

The deputy sobered. He crowded close to Wade McMasters as though seeking protection from the fierce, hollow-eyed figure glaring at him.

"Sure I tore it up!" he said, with a sudden display of bravado. "I sure did. . . ."

"I'm sorry, Marshal," Parmalee broke through the grief and blinding fury that gripped Sutton. "If I'd known. . . . Stalled long as I could, but when you didn't show up—and we didn't hear—"

"Tore up his letter, Wade," the deputy chanted. "Kept him from writing the judge. . . . Had to have us a sucker. Harp and Stinger's dead . . . shot 'em both. But Stinger talked anyway. . . . Dead—"

Jack Sutton's head came up slowly, his narrowed eyes reaching for McMasters. The sheriff's face was taut. Color was draining away.

"We're going to have to kill him, too, Wade!" Gerlay yelled suddenly, pointing at Sutton. "Knows

184

all about us—and he'll be doggin' us rest of our days. He's that kind. . . . Shoot him—Wade!"

For an instant Sutton remained motionless, stunned by the deputy's words. McMasters was in on it, too! And he, most of all, could have interceded for Billy— saved him from the gallows. Instead, he had stood there and watched him die. Rage flared through Jack Sutton. He spun, jerking his rifle from its boot.

McMasters fired as Sutton whirled back. The bullet sliced across the muscles of Jack's arm. He dropped to his knees, levered two quick shots while the echoes were still rolling. McMasters staggered, dropped his pistol and clawed at his chest.

Gerlay yelled and grabbed at the lawman's revolver. Sutton fired again; he saw the deputy's face disappear into a mass of blood.

"Great God!" Henry Parmalee's voice, penetrating the coiling smoke, sounded high, unnatural.

Sutton leaned weakly against the cross bar of the hitchrack. Blood dripped steadily from his elbow, fell into the dust.

In the continuing hush Parmalee said, "I—I'm sorry about this—all of it. Whole town is. . . . If there's anything I—we—can do—"

Jack Sutton raised his lean face. Pure hatred glowed in his sunken eyes and his mouth was pulled into an ugly snarl as he swept the crowd with a slow, contemptuous glance that halted on the jurist.

"Fry in hell—that's what you can do for me," he grated, and turning, climbed onto his horse and rode off.

EPILOGUE

Henry Parmalee's prophecy came true.
Seven years later, almost to the day, the railroad pushed its way down the beautiful Valley of the Conquerors, laying its steel path upon the same ground helmeted soldiers had trod some three hundred years before.

But the shining ribbons never came to Trailbreak. The necessity for reaching lands beyond by the shortest route brought about a change in the original plans, and the tracks curved westward, missing the waiting settlement by a long ten miles.

Ignored, isolated, the town began to wither. One by one families moved away. Storekeepers closed their doors, and carted their stocks to other, more promising points. Mysteriously, the bank burned to its foundation. Ranchers began to avoid the place, took their business to the brawling new town that sprang into being even before the gandy dancers had sledged their last spikes into the still green ties.

Thus, because it was shunned, the town died. But there were those who thought otherwise. Trailbreak was dead long before the coming of the clattering steam wagons; Trailbreak died, they said, in a blaze of gunfire and a flood of shame one hot August noon—died with a hangman's curse upon its head.

And so now the lonely wind moves restlessly through deserted streets and empty buildings searching, perhaps, for men who will never return. Like those men, the wind looked upon violence that blistering hour and was appalled. . . . Unlike those men, the wind can never forget, for it lives on forever.

Center Point Publishing
600 Brooks Road ● PO Box 1
Thorndike ME 04986-0001 USA

(207) 568-3717

US & Canada:
1 800 929-9108